"JM Tohline's first novel, *The Great Lenore*, is a beautiful book. It is beautiful in the same way that J.D. Salinger's books are beautiful. Lyrical without being pretentious or self absorbed, melodic without being baroque, it is refreshing in the same way a fortunate musical composition hangs in your consciousness after the last note has sounded, making it impossible for long moments to think. One just feels."

~ Jeremy McGuire, The New York Journal of Books

the

great

lenore

the

great

lenore

a novel

j m

tohline

An Atticus Trade Paperback Original

Atticus Books LLC
3766 Howard Avenue, Suite 202
Kensington MD 20895
http://atticusbooksonline.com

ISBN-13: 978-0-9845105-5-9
ISBN-10: 0-9845105-5-9

Typeset in Minion
Cover design by Jamie Keenan

Author photo: Abby E Marrero

Acknowledgements

Mom and Dad, thank you. For everything. Your support and belief has been a thing of beauty. Stephanie and Lauren, thank you for loving me endlessly. I'm so proud of you both. Abby, thank you for being my sunlight. Kolodziejs, thank you for giving me a beautiful haven for writing, and for always expecting this day to come. Arbos, thank you for encouraging all of us to follow our dreams, no matter how strange they might be. To the family, friends, and men of Cov who I do not have the space to mention: Thank you, thank you, thank you.

An Important Note to the Reader

I once listened to an interview with a popular author-who-shall-remain-nameless, in which he complained about people who tell him, "I love your books! I've loaned them to all my friends." In the interview, this author said something along the lines of: "I don't get paid if you loan my books to your friends. Tell your friends to buy them!"

Let me diverge from that story, and let's talk about the topic at hand—that is, the book that you are holding.

Dear Reader, if you buy one copy of this book and loan it to your entire family—thank you.

If you buy a copy for yourself and a copy to loan, and you loan that extra copy to fifty people who never purchase the book themselves, thank you.

If you read this book and it makes you fly and you tell others about it, you have my eternal gratitude.

To all of you who love reading—to all of you who spread the love of reading—thank you.

And of course, to each of you who is willing to give a new author a slice of your attention in spite of your busy schedule, I cannot thank you enough.

This book is for you.

Dear Reader,
Read this and fly.

Ah, broken is the golden bowl! the spirit flown forever!
Let the bell toll!—a saintly soul floats on the Stygian river;
And, Guy De Vere, hast thou no tear?—weep now or never more!
See! on yon drear and rigid bier low lies thy love, Lenore!
Come! let the burial rite be read—the funeral song be sung!—
An anthem for the queenliest dead that ever died so young—
A dirge for her, the doubly dead in that she died so young.

~ Edgar Allen Poe, "Lenore"

Life is life and fun is fun, but it is always so quiet
when the gold fish die.

~ Beryl Markham, *West with the Night*

CHAPTER 1

When I met Lenore, she'd been dead for four days.

"I'm so sorry," she said. She stood on the back patio with water dripping from her hair. She looked cold. "I feel awful for barging in like this, I hope I'm not being a bother. I couldn't go next door, you know."

"I know," I said.

The Atlantic stretched out behind her like an angry black sheet. The rain chased itself into the water.

"Oh, I'm sorry. Here." She held out her hand. "I'm Lenore."

"Lenore. Right."

Her eyes kissed mine as she brushed past me.

I opened my mouth to say something. Nothing.

Lenore reached the fireplace, and she plucked the poker up from beside the brick façade and stuck it into the dying embers. Ashes rose. The coals glowed brighter.

"Is there any more wood?" she said. Her voice was mesmerizing. The British accent lingered in the air long after the words faded. She had to repeat her question before I realized what she had asked.

"Yeah, sure. Sure," I said. "I'll run out and get some."

I returned from outside with two fresh logs—rain sliding down my face, the cold pounding inside my chest—and Lenore was sitting in front of the fireplace, wrapped in a blanket. Her smile left my legs in desperate need of strength. I reached the fireplace and let the logs tumble in amongst the coals.

"Thank you, Richard—you really are a sweetheart. Come down here and let me kiss you."

I bent down close to her, and she placed her fingers on my chin and tilted my face. Her lips touched my forehead. The flames licked the wood.

* * *

I learned a long time ago that people gravitate toward Mystery.

I'm not much of a mysterious man myself—not in my own estimation, at least. I'm really very much normal. But over the years I've discovered that many people mistake me for mysterious, and this misconception has led me into some strange friendships.

Fittingly, it was one such friendship that began this whole story—my friendship with Sandy Banucci.

I met Sandy during my freshman year of college. He was my roommate that year, and for two other years also, and he was the opposite of me in every way imaginable.

While I preferred thought over noise, Sandy preferred to be loud and obnoxious and utterly unambitious. And while I had all the social aspirations of a hermit, Sandy was gregarious and likeable, and he became popular around campus. I probably would have hated college if not for our friendship. He made me feel alive.

One of the habits that Sandy picked up during our first year together—endlessly annoying, but creating great results—was a tendency to drag me places and introduce me to his friends.

"This is my roommate Richard," he used to say. "Doesn't he look *exactly* like Denzel Washington?"

I don't look *exactly* like Denzel Washington. But that was *exactly* how he always introduced me.

Since that time, a lot in my life has changed, but one thing that hasn't changed is Sandy. Even after I got to be—well, I wouldn't really call myself famous, but we'll say 'well-known'— even after I got to be well-known, Sandy was still the same. I was still his "good buddy Richard, doesn't he look *exactly* like Denzel Washington," and he was still old sandy-haired Sandy.

It was in the fall of last year that he called me and began this whole story.

"Rich," he said to me, as soon as I said Hello, "my family is wintering in Europe this year—out in Germany, or some crap like that. Gonna study up our roots. Anyhow, I was thinking the other day and I thought I could do you a favor."

"A favor?"

"Exactly. Look, we have that beach house out on Nantucket, right? But none of us are gonna get any use out of it this winter—you know, we'll all be out in Hitler's backyard. And what I realized is: I hate for the place to go to waste all winter. And didn't you say something about writing your next novel? Seems like I remember that. And I thought you'd maybe enjoy staying out there for the winter. For part of the winter, at least. Just sort of look after the place and enjoy it."

I had no plans for the winter, and Sandy was right about me looking for a place where I could relax and be away from it all and work on my next novel, so I told him it all sounded like a pretty good idea. We worked out the details, and I flew into Boston on Friday, the twenty-first of November.

Sandy picked me up at the airport that evening, and that night we crashed with Shannon—an old friend of ours from Fairfield who was playing house in a small town outside the city with a nice guy named Guy from upstate New York. We had a pleasant time with Shannon and Guy—Shannon cooked dinner, they shared their wine with us, Guy showed us his license plate collection and his "skills" on the electric guitar ("It's just a hobby," he told us, as he slung the strap over his head, "just a hobby, you know, but I enjoy it")—and it was nice to see her and fine to meet him. But . . . really, I was ready to get to Nantucket. I wanted to settle in. I wanted to begin writing.

I figured we would head to Nantucket when we woke up on Saturday, but when we woke up on Saturday we headed into the city.

"I want you to meet my good buddy Maxwell," Sandy said.

"Sandy, really? Can't we just—"

"Come on, Rich. You'll like this guy."

"Sandy—"

"You *will*. What? You'll like him, Rich—I'm absolutely certain."

Honestly, it all seemed like more trouble than it was worth—battling the traffic, getting flipped off by strangers, narrowly avoiding car wrecks and wrecks with pedestrians. Looking back, it's funny in that "Yeah, it's catastrophic and all you can do is laugh" sort of way. That introduction to Maxwell was so catalytic, and yet . . . it seemed so unexceptional at the time.

This is what the scene looked like when we arrived at Maxwell's apartment in the Back Bay in Boston:

Sandy knocked, and the door flew open.

Maxwell stood in the doorway wearing a Beatles T-shirt, ripped jeans, and a magnanimous smile—the kind of mischievous, childlike smile that makes women go all weak—and smoke curled from a cigarette in one hand, and he held a glass of scotch in the other.

"Sandy! Hahaaaa!" Both men yelled and embraced like kids, and a sliver of scotch leaped from the glass and landed on

Sandy's shoulder. Neither man noticed. They let go of each other and shoved their way back into the apartment.

"Here's my buddy Richard," Sandy said, struggling out of his coat.

"Richard. How are you, brother. I'm Maxwell." Maxwell shifted the cigarette to his mouth and offered me his hand. I gripped it tight. Looked him in his eyes.

"A pleasure to meet you," I told him. "You have a lovely place here."

"Whoa, whoaaaa," Maxwell said, and he laughed, and he removed the cigarette and slurped a messy sip from the glass. "Where'd you find this cat, huh, Sandy? 'Pleasure to meet you'? 'Lovely place'? C'mon, brother,"—he slapped my shoulder— "lighten up a bit, huh?" He turned without noticing the scathing look I gave him, and he drifted deeper into his sumptuous, softly-lit apartment. "When are you flying out, anyway?" he called to Sandy.

I heard bottles clanking in some invisible corner of the apartment, and Sandy returned with two bottles in one hand and two glasses in the other.

"Where the hell's your ice, ol' Max?"

Maxwell plopped down on the couch. He pointed vaguely. "Back in the bar, didn't you see it? I got this new ice-maker installed, just above the sink." Sandy disappeared again, and Maxwell patted the couch. "Sit down," he said to me. "You smoke?"

I chose a different chair, on the opposite wall, and I eased into it slowly.

"Sure," he said, "sit over there. That's fine too."

Maxwell stubbed out his cigarette in an ashtray that was shaped like an upturned turtle shell, then he gulped more alcohol and lit a new cigarette.

"Richy," he said. He blew smoke at the ceiling. "If you could choose one Hollywood chick to get with, who would it be?"

"I, um . . ."

Sandy came back into the room and handed me a glass.

I looked at my watch, then I shrugged and took a sip.

"So, Max," Sandy said, and he sat beside Maxwell. "You'll never guess who I hooked up with last weekend. Go on, have a guess."

"I don't know."

"Just have a *guess*."

"Two-Tooth Tammy."

"Aw, c'mon!"

"Look, I don't give a damn," Maxwell said. He looked at me and smiled. "Sandy's always trying to brag about these girls he hooks up with. But I'm telling you right now, half his stories are lies."

"Lies my ass! Hey, look at Richard. Tell me who he looks like."

Maxwell drank his drink and pointed at me with his cigarette. "Richy, have you ever gone Date Popping?"

"Doesn't he look *exactly* like Denzel Washington?"

"He doesn't look a damn sight like Denzel Washington!"

I took a sip of my drink.

We drank a lot that night. We drank too much, in fact, and then we marched raucously into the streets of Boston and began playing what Maxwell referred to as "Social Sports" (the particular Social Sport of the evening being what Maxwell called Date Popping, which involves stumbling intoxicated into restaurants and trying to break up dates by pretending to be a jealous lover or an angry sibling or some sort of past-life embarrassment), and by the time I dropped Sandy off at the airport on Sunday and moved to Nantucket for what I thought would be "for good" (or, at least, "for the winter") I was desperately happy to be there at last. And I desperately needed sleep.

I slept all evening and all night on Sunday, and on Monday morning I awoke feeling refreshed. I brewed a pot of coffee, and I sat on the back patio.

The crisp air slicing off the ocean.

The contemplative mornings.

I miss those things about Banucci Manor. I miss a lot of things, actually—the stateliness, the beauty, the everything-about-it. I miss the quiet magnificence. I miss the understated majesty.

Banucci Manor rests along the eastern shoreline of Nantucket—on some of America's most exclusive real estate—and it rests there as if resting exactly where it belongs. There is no self-consciousness about Banucci Manor's perfection. There is nothing about the house or the view or the landscaping that says, "Look at us, we're rich and important! We're trying really hard." The house is massive, and its grounds are like heaven. The view could knock you out even if you saw it every day. And nothing about it seems remotely out of place.

Of course, there is plenty that I do not miss about Banucci Manor as well. There is plenty that I think about whenever I think about that place that makes me wish I had never gone there.

At the time, however, everything seemed promising. Everything seemed unwritten.

Ha!—*Unwritten.*

I feel like an old man right now, reminiscing over a long-dead past. But the past that I am remembering has barely begun to decompose. The past that I am remembering continues to seep into my present.

I laugh at the word "Unwritten" because, quite simply, had I been *able* to write while I was on Nantucket (after all, that's what I went there for in the first place), I might have kept my nose where it belonged. That is, confined to my own business. But ahhh (deep breath), my lot was not so lucky.

I was unable to write on my first morning at Banucci Manor, and so I explored the house. I explored the grounds. I continued to drink mugs full of coffee (which, in time, became glasses full of whiskey), and I sat on the back patio and watched the grass that undulated like wind-tickled water until it bumped into sand, and the sand fell down into the ocean. I thought my thoughts, and I awaited inspiration.

I spent a lot of time outside during that day and the next. Ideas and inspiration continued to elude me, but I didn't so much mind. At the time, it was pleasant—I slipped from an envious possession of Banucci Manor into a homesteader's proud occupation.

One thing that particularly caught my critical eye during this time, as I began to think of Banucci Manor in terms of *mine* and began to judge and belittle both the abodes and the lives of others, was the house just south of Banucci Manor—a garish and tasteless affair that I referred to from the outset as The Palace.

The Palace was overlarge. It was gaudy. By the end of my first day at Banucci Manor I began to glance toward The Palace periodically with a distaste that bordered on rancor, and I wondered what sort of awful people must live there. At times (often at my drunkest) I simply watched The Palace as if waiting for it to mobilize itself, whereupon it would likely begin to attack the homes and land around it.

On Tuesday—my second full day on Nantucket, and still unable to write—I sat on the back patio of Banucci Manor in the afternoon, drinking whiskey and staring across the Atlantic and trying my damndest to ignore the leering bulk of The Palace on the periphery. Wind gushed off the face of the water, and I heard a car door shut.

I stood.

I set the whiskey on the table beside me. I stretched my arms and legs. I looked at the ocean, for no reason other than that the ocean was spectacular, and I leaned around the corner of the patio, around the corner of the house. I gazed across the day.

The sun trickled down through the clouds in droplet-sized pieces.

The day was gorgeous, and the grass unfolded like a big green blanket.

There were two cars in the driveway of The Palace, all abuzz with life.

I leaned forward.

There was a woman on the front walk of The Palace.

As I was standing so far away (and was wearing a rather thick pair of whiskey goggles to boot), it was difficult to tell exactly what the woman looked like—but I got the impression that she was a young woman, and that she was absolutely stunning. And that her hair was probably red. She walked like an angel and looked like an angel, and when she reached the front porch of The Palace she stopped and pushed her hair back and turned, and she called to someone at the cars.

From the other side of the cars, I heard a voice answer. A man's voice.

I watched.

The day watched.

The whole world watched.

The man appeared from around the side of the cars—a big man, with hulking shoulders and a cruel, muscular body.

The girl didn't hear his answer, and he answered her again.

I didn't move. I kept watching.

It looked like the girl sighed, like maybe she turned around with a huff, and she slipped inside of The Palace.

The big muscular man followed from the cars.

I watched, and more people followed from the cars:

A young man, hair placed impeccably, dressed like a 1920s businessman.

Two older people.

Maxwell.

Maxwell!—I thought. I took a step back. Is that Maxwell? Watching.

Thinking.

I picked up my whiskey.

Perhaps I already knew that Maxwell's family owned The Palace, but if I knew...I certainly did not remember.

I took a sip of my whiskey.

Perhaps that's something Sandy had told me, sometime after he introduced me to Maxwell. If that's something he had told me...

* * *

The sun is also rising, outside of my window, piercing the blinds and stretching itself in thin lines across the cold, wooden floor.

I am sitting at an ill-lit desk in a flat above the left bank of the Seine River, near the spot where Ernest Hemingway wrote his second novel. I have been living here for a couple weeks. The flat is bare and ugly.

One of my neighbors has a baby that sleeps during the day, and it wakes up at nighttime to cry and cry.

Across the way, there is a dog who waits at a slat in the gate and barks at every passerby. The road carries a lot of foot traffic, and people pass the dog all day.

I don't know many people here. Not yet. I don't know the language too well.

Sometimes, I feel lonely. And...as was the case during my time on Nantucket, I have been unable to write.

However, I am no longer on Nantucket. I am an ocean away. This, at least, is one thing for which I can be happy.

* * *

On Wednesday afternoon—now halfway through my third full day on Nantucket—I sat at the desk in the downstairs study and drank whiskey while I stared at my computer. Nothing came to me, no matter how long I waited.

The doorbell rang.

I continued to stare at my computer, as if something would somehow change.

The doorbell rang again.

I slammed my computer shut.

I took a gulp of my whiskey.

I banged the glass down onto the table.

The doorbell rang a third time.

I stood from my chair and stood still for a moment to make certain I had my balance and I made my way to the foyer with the gracious help of the walls. I pulled the door open. I peered out into the world.

Standing there on my own front porch and looking endlessly uncomfortable was the hulking brute from the next house over.

"Hey," he said.

"Hi."

"I, uh . . ." he looked to his right, at the house from which he'd just come. "I'm Chas. Maxwell's brother." He held out his hand. I gripped it tight. Looked him in his eyes. "You mind if I come in?"

Allow me to interject an admission about myself—and I admit this, largely, because this might save me trouble in the future if you and I ever have the (*cough*) fortune of running into one another: I judge most people the moment I meet them. And most often, I don't like what I see.

It's a flaw of mine, I know.

On that day on Nantucket, I stood in the darkness of the foyer wearing jeans and a sweater and an old fedora I had picked up at a thrift store five years earlier, and I faced this handsome, overly-buff young man standing in the sun with a CEO's haircut and slacks and a dress shirt, and he had asked me: 'You mind if I come in?'

Inside my head, I said, "Yes, I do mind. Of course I mind! Look, I don't really like you. I just met you, and I don't really like you."

But out loud: "Oh, sure. Sure, come on in."

I kept my hand on the wall again and tried to walk steady, and I led Chas to the living room and sat down in the salmon-colored chair by the window. I offered him a seat.

He didn't take it.

He stood there with his hands in his pockets and his eyes wandering all over the room. "I just came over to see if you'd like to join us tomorrow, for Thanksgiving. When—" He cleared his throat. "Sorry. Um...oh, yes—when Mamma found out you were over here by yourself, she couldn't stand the thought."

"Mmm, oh. Yeah?" My tongue felt thick inside my mouth.

"Yes," he said, and his eyes continued to wander all over the room. "It's important to her that you come."

"Mmm..."

Chas left, and I stood in the doorway and watched him. He strode all the way up the driveway of Banucci Manor and along the road until he reached the driveway of The Palace, then he descended upon its absurd luxuriousness from above, as if it would have been too terribly mundane and common to have tramped across the grass.

I shook my head.

I returned to my desk and opened my computer and stared at my computer. I set my hands on the keyboard, then I sipped my drink and returned my hands to the keyboard and continued to watch the screen.

"Dammit," I said. I closed the computer again.

I sat on the back patio and watched the ocean—which continued to do the same thing it had been doing for the last three days—and I continued to sip my whiskey and to let my mind wander.

My mind came around to some sort of opalescent memory. Boston—I could very nearly see it. Boston, the morning after Sandy and Maxwell and I drank too much and wandered hooligan-like around the city Popping Dates.

Sandy and Maxwell and I sat by the window of a sidewalk café, playing around with plates full of food. I still felt drunk from the previous night's escapades of excess, and Sandy and Maxwell talked.

"How's your brother doing?" Sandy said. He was looking at no one, but Maxwell answered.

"My brother? He's still a royal asshole, if that's what you're asking."

"That's what I figured," Sandy said. He laughed. "What's the deal with him, anyway?"

"Whaddaya mean?"

"What do I...I don't know what I mean. Ha, I'm sort of stoned."

"Yeah?"

Sandy nodded.

"Yeah, brother—me too."

Sandy laughed again.

Both guys looked at me and raised their eyebrows. Their faces asked if I was stoned also.

I shook my head.

They turned back to one another.

"Is your brother still dating that one girl?" Sandy asked. He picked up his sandwich and set it back down.

"He—is he still *dating* her? He married her."

"No—no, not . . . Lenore. I was at that wedding, remember? I don't mean Lenore. I mean the girl he's *dating*."

"Oh. I don't know."

People walked past the window, on the sidewalk. I remember I watched the people. I ate my sandwich, and I listened to Sandy and Maxwell.

"You don't know?" Sandy said.

"No. I try and stay out of all that. I try and just—you know—ignore."

"I hear you. She's damn good-looking. What's her name?"

"Who?"

"The girl who Chas is dating."

"Oh, her. Yeah, her name is Lily."

"Lily, that's right. Lily. She's damn good-looking," Sandy said.

"It's Chas," Maxwell said. He scratched his face. "Of course she's good-looking."

Sandy stared into his sandwich as though it held some sort of secret. When he looked back up he asked for a cigarette. Maxwell handed him one. "Yeah," Sandy said. He lit the cigarette. "Ol' Chas." He blew out smoke. "What a royal asshole . . . "

I continued to sit outside on the back patio of Banucci Manor, thinking about this and eventually thinking about other things instead. I stood only periodically, only to stumble inside and refill my drink or relieve myself in the bathroom.

The sun set behind me, and the titanic house blocked the sun so that twilight swirled around me for a while and made the world look soft. The ocean looked pale. The ocean kept moving and making noise, and I sipped my drink and lulled down inside of everything and time slipped past me, warm and fluent.

Maxwell stalked across the grass that night and hailed me from too far away for me to hear what he said.

I looked up. I watched him walk toward me.

When he reached the back patio, he sat. He grabbed my whiskey and took a big gulp. He set the glass down and thanked me.

I said: "Yup."

Maxwell said: "Yeah . . ."

Both of us said nothing.

The sky was clear that night—clear and cold. An ocean sky. A New England sky. Maxwell and I continued to say nothing, and finally he pulled out a joint, and we started to smoke it in silence.

"Good God," Maxwell said finally, and he held the smoke in his lungs. "Where's the dynamite, huh?"

My arm moved away from me, slooowly. I grabbed the joint from Maxwell and searched for my mouth.

"Damn," Maxwell said.

I said nothing.

The joint disappeared from my fingers and floated. Smoke escaped my mouth. I took a sip of whiskey.

"What time . . . are . . . you coming over tomorrow anyway?"

I didn't answer.

"Duuude," Maxwell said.

I pinched the joint between my fingers, careful not to burn my skin.

"Hey," Maxwell said. "Hey, heeey. Dude, hey. How much of a bitch is my brother, huh? Man, what a bitch. You know." He pointed the joint at me. He finished it. Killed it beneath his foot. "I really don't know *how* he got Lenore. Boy, that boggles my mind, brother. My *mind*." Maxwell pointed at his mind.

Whoosh, Whoosh!

I listened to the water.

Whoosh, Whoosh!

Neither of us spoke. Neither of us needed to. We waited for absolutely nothing.

Whoosh, Wh—

"Hey," Maxwell said. I looked at him. "You wanna smoke another one?"

Maxwell and I either smoked another joint or we didn't—I don't remember—and then we moved inside. I sat in the salmon-colored chair by the window, and Maxwell laid across the couch that I'd offered to his brother earlier in the day.

Somewhere, a clock ticked. Somewhere, time disappeared. Both of us stared at separate spots on the wall and swam through the morass of our drug-addled brains, and we sat so close to one another, and we drifted through worlds that were so far apart.

I dozed off for a bit.

Maxwell woke me with this:

"What the hell was she thinking?"

I sat there slumped in the chair. I said nothing, but Maxwell said nothing also, so finally I just said, "Who knows."

"My brother is such a prick," he told the wall. "*Such* a prick. Like, I mean. He doesn't even care about her. I'm not saying *I* care. I don't. You know?"

"Of course not."

"But I'm just saying." He reached for his drink. "Say," he said, "what'd he say to you this afternoon?"

"Nothing." I closed my eyes and opened them again. It took effort. "He didn't say much," I said. "He just … stopped by, really. Said he hates your rotten guts."

Maxwell's drink spurted out of his mouth in a spray of laughter. "He probably did, man—he probably *did* say that. I'm not kidding, ha!" Somewhere, a clock ticked. Somewhere, time disappeared, building a mountain beneath us like so many grains of sand. A mountain on which we all stand, which is always growing, always growing higher. A mountain down the side of which no one will ever descend. "He tell you to come over tomorrow?"

"He told me that your mom couldn't *staaand* the thought of me being here all alone."

Maxwell laughed again, and more alcohol was wasted. "Wait'll you meet my mom, man. Hey, *hey*." He leaned over the edge of the couch, and his fingers brushed the ground. He looked at me—or, at least, he tried to. "Wanna know what my mom's gonna say, huh? The moment you meet her?"

I shrugged.

"The moment you meet her—I'm not kidding, 'kay? I absolutely promise—the moment you meet her and say, whatever, say 'Hi Mrs. Montana, nice to make your acquaintance,' or whatever the hell it is that someone like you'll say, she'll shake your hand all jolly-like, and she'll smile real big and go, 'Oh, dear, I'm just *thrilled* to meet you. Call me Mamma, okay? That's what they *all* call me, Mamma Montana.' I swear to it, man. It's the way it goes every damn time. The corniest thing you ever saw."

"That doesn't sound so bad."

"Doesn't sound so bad!" Maxwell tried to sit. He gave up after a couple seconds and his head lolled back down onto the cushions. He fidgeted his fingers. "Doesn't sound so bad, huh? Hmph. It's all a big act, man. That's all it is. I bet . . . man, I bet they even planned it, even. That's what I think. Like, for business and all. Dad plays the stoic gentleman, and Mom plays the matronly . . . wife. The matronly mother, whatever." His voice began to trail off, as if he thought about something else. "And it works, man. That's the crazy damn thing—it absolutely *works*. For years it has. Anytime anyone comes home to the house, Dad's all the strong big boss. Whatever. And she's all 'Mamma Montana.' Hell," he said. He looked at the floor. His words became thinner. "I'm surprised she didn't go and put on about a hundred pounds to make herself look like Old Mother Hen. Some shit like that. I guess she couldn't go *that* far, though. You know. She also's gotta look the part of The Rich Executive's Wife. Or whatever."

"It doesn't sound so bad," I said again.

"Believe me," he said. "It is."

He rolled back over. Buried his face in the couch.

If I had to guess, I would tell you this: Maxwell probably was no longer in that room with me at all. He probably had his eyes closed, and he was thinking about Lenore.

CHAPTER 2

"Oh, dear, I'm just *thrilled* to meet you."

"The pleasure is all mine."

"Call me Mamma, okay? That's what they *all* call me, Mamma Montana."

"Mamma Montana. I like that." I did like it. It didn't seem so bad. It seemed contrived, sure. It seemed insincere. But it seemed . . . it seemed to fit her. Like she was contrivable. Like she was insincere. Like that was all okay.

"Sorry I'm such a mess!" she said, and she pushed her hair off her face. "I've been up since practically *sun*rise, slaving away in the kitchen!"

Actually, Mamma Montana didn't look a mess at all. That's what I told her.

"Oh, you're just *too* sweet!"

In fact, she looked downright stunning.

In fact, she looked about the way you would *expect* a woman to look who hasn't had a worry in the world for the last thirty years.

She and I stood in the kitchen speaking in perfunctories for maybe about a minute, then Mamma Montana reached up and set her hands on my shoulders. "Sweetheart, the men are in the drawing room, okay? You go settle in with them, and we'll chat later." She hugged me. She kissed me on the cheek.

The drawing room faced the ocean, and the sun poured in through a full wall of windows, painting the floor and chairs and walls a soft, clean yellow. A piano stood in one corner of the drawing room, full of pretension and looking like it hadn't been played in decades. Books decorated the wall across from the windows—leatherbound books, likely unread, perhaps printed specifically to fill these bookshelves, and the bookshelves having perhaps been built for the express purpose of housing these particular books.

When my feet hit the hardwood floor, Chas glanced at me and kept his seat. Two other men stood, and they introduced themselves in turn.

"Mr. Montana," the first one said. I gripped his hand tight. Looked him in his eyes.

Whenever I meet new people, I study them—that's the first thing I do. I take everything in, and I process. I make assumptions.

As I said before—I decide whether I like the person or not.

Mr. Montana had a hard, empty face, and he looked strong and healthy and successful. He looked formidable. He looked like the kind of man who would slice your throat open if he had to, but who also paid little enough attention to the people around him to ever notice if he had to. He was a two dimensional man, and these two dimensions were: Himself and His Money.

I turned.

"I'm Jez," the second man said. I gripped his hand tight. Looked him in his eyes.

Jez was the young man I'd seen entering The Palace two days earlier—the one who looked like a 1920's businessman. Today he wore light cotton slacks and a starched black shirt. His hair was slicked back. His teeth and lips and skin—everything about him, actually—were absolutely impeccable. His face betrayed nothing about him. I let go of his hand and kept looking at him and knew absolutely nothing.

The three of us sat.

The men picked up their drinks.

The chairs were set up in a semi-circle around a coffee table, and we faced the grass and the ocean and sun beyond the wall of windows, sitting like this: Me, Mr. Montana, Jez, Chas.

"What I was saying—" Mr. Montana said; he turned to look at me. "Before you came in, see, we were discussing the pitfalls of the current financial landscape—" I returned his look and nodded, "and I think that there's an upswing on the horizon in the technology sector. Chas here, though..." Mr. Montana stopped. I stared at the back of his head. "Chas. Did you not offer our guest here a drink?"

"I...no. I didn't think of it."

"My apologies," Mr. Montana said. He swung his head toward me. "My boy never picked up on the manners we tried to teach him as a kid. Now, what would you like to drink?"

"Oh, I'm fine. Don't worry about—"

"No, no. I insist."

I glanced over Mr. Montana's shoulder and saw Jez pick up his drink and sample it and set it back down. His eyes seemed to stare unseeing through the window, as though the serene smile on his face had nothing to do with the day or the surroundings or any other external factors. He looked neither rude nor overconfident, but rather as though it was up to him to bestow his attention upon or withhold his attention from anything that was said.

"Think about it a moment," Mr. Montana said, "you can have what you'd like. We have brandy, whiskey, wine—well, I believe we're saving the wine for dinner—scotch, but you get the picture. You can have what you'd like. Me, I always drink bourbon. Nothing but bourbon for me." He reached forward and picked up his glass and rattled it so the ice clinked. He took a large sip—a gulp, I guess—and he continued. "What I was saying, though—" and he interrupted himself to knock back another mouthful of bourbon, then he set the glass down and, *Ahh, that's good*, continued as if he'd never stopped, "is that you have to look at the patterns. We're in the fifth cycle right now, right?" He pointed at me. I had no clue what he was saying, but I nodded. "Which puts the third cycle—technology and telecommunications—on the opposite side of the wheel. Why, you know, of course: Buy low, sell high—it's the only principle to live off. And that's the only way to tell when something *is* low. Look at the wheel."

"I'm not saying the wheel doesn't *work*," Chas said, "I just think that the technology sector still has a little ways to fall befo—"

"You decide on a drink yet, son?"

"Oh. I, um . . ." I shook my head. Mr. Montana was looking at me again. "Yessir, sure. I guess I'll take a whiskey. With ice."

"Chas," Mr. Montana said, his head swiveling, "get this young man a drink." Swivel. "What's your whiskey of choice, son?"

"Jack. Um, if you have it."

"Get him a Jack—on the rocks."

Chas stood. He started to leave the room.

"Sorry about my boy's manners," Mr. Montana said. "He just never quite learned."

Mr. Montana began talking again, and Jez listened.

Chas returned with my drink.

I looked at my watch, then I shrugged and took a sip.

I contributed little to the conversation that morning, but I'm quite certain Mr. Montana didn't notice. He prattled on and the other two nodded, and occasionally Jez spoke up and Mr. Montana nodded, and occasionally Mr. Montana looked at me and I nodded also. Anytime when I wasn't nodding, I sank into the softness of the world outside the window. I watched the way the sunlight hit the trees in their garden and broke everything apart. I watched the ocean moving and the grass moving in the wind. I appreciated the beauty of Nantucket in a way I doubted these three men had appreciated it in ages.

About an hour later Maxwell puttered around the corner, wearing skivvies and an undershirt, and he passed through the drawing room and flipped me off and smiled and slipped into the kitchen.

He sprinted from the kitchen a few seconds later, laughing under a deluge of shrieked reproaches from Mamma Montana— "Make yourself decent before you come down here again!"

Maxwell returned after another half hour and put his hand on my shoulder and squeezed and told me to join him outside. I excused myself from the men and followed him to the back porch.

"What a colossal *bore*, huh? Good Gaaawd!"

He slumped down into a white wicker chair. His shirt and pants were slightly wrinkled. The sun bounced off his face to highlight his two-or-three-day stubble.

Maxwell's hair (greasy blond, just *barely* too short to make a decent ponytail) was pushed back off his face. He wore flip-flops. It was thirty-five degrees outside.

He stretched his legs out in front of him and stretched his arms toward the ocean. He looked up at me. "I bet you're wondering where Lenore is, huh?"

"Lenore?"

"*Lenore*," he said, and he said it as if I was stupid for not knowing what he was talking about. He slipped a cigarette from his pocket. "My brother's *wife*."

"Oh. Right."

"Right." He lit the cigarette and started smoking.

"What was your question?"

"Why don't you sit down, brother."

"Okay," I said. I sat down beside him.

"Lenore. Haven't you wondered where she is?"

"Oh. Not really, I—"

"She's back in London."

"Okay."

"Yeah, poor Chas. You know, I think she might be tired of him. Getting tired of him, at least. She stayed here in Nantucket for most of the summer."

"Lenore did?"

Maxwell nodded. He eased his arms up over his head. Cracked his knuckles. Pulled the cigarette from his lips and puffed a cloud of smoke.

"What is she doing in London?" I asked.

"Visiting her grandpa, probably. I don't know. That's where she's from, you know."

"Oh." That was all I said.

"Yeahhh, Lenore. I guess her grandpa is pretty important over there, or something. Some shit like that. Supposed to be filthy rich, too."

"Yeah?"

"Yeah, of course. Not like it matters to me or anything, but I figured you might be wondering where she is—I mean, she is my brother's wife and all."

"Uh-huh. I don't know who she is, really. So—"

"Sandy and I were talking about her. You remember that, don't you? Yeah, you remember that. We were talking about how Chas is dating that girl Lily. She's pretty cute—Lily. Chas is dating her, right? But he's married to Lenore. Anyhow, I just figured you probably remembered us talking about that. I figured you were probably wondering."

"I sort of remember that now."

"I'll tell you, if Cecilia ever finds out that Chas is cheating on Lenore, brother, she'll throw a fit. An absolute fit."

"Cecilia?"

"My *sister*. You haven't met Cecilia?"

"I—"

"You will," he said.

"Of course."

"Of course. Yeah." The wind threw itself at our faces. Maxwell finished his cigarette. He crushed it beneath his foot. "How about Jez? You met him, right?"

"I met Jez. I was just sitting in there with him."

"Right. Okay."

We watched the waves in the distance.

I thought of Jez. I saw him inside my mind. I saw his gorgeous face and his flawless sense of unadorned style. I saw his demeanor—knowledgeable. I saw his confidence—impeccable. I saw his calm outer shell of unselfconscious success.

I turned toward Maxwell and his disheveled appearance. "What's the story with Jez, anyway?" I said.

Maxwell stretched his arms over his head. He cracked his knuckles again, first on one hand, then on the other. "How do you mean?"

"How . . . well, who is he? Where'd he come from? Is he just an employee of your dad's? Or what?"

Maxwell reached into his pocket. "Sort of." He pulled out a new cigarette. Lit it. Picked up my drink and took a big gulp.

"Sort of?" I said.

"Sort of." He sucked the life out his cigarette and released smoke into the air where it disappeared forever.

I waited.

He smoked.

He started talking.

He explained about himself, and about his brother, and about Jez.

In high school, Maxwell scored twenty points shy of perfect on his SAT—and he never studied for it once. Maxwell had scholarship offers to just about every school in the country—to schools he never even applied to. Maxwell's Harvard professors called him 'One of the brightest young men to ever attend the college.'

Of course, this was before he almost got kicked out for all the Social Sports he organized and hosted each weekend—events like Date Popping, like Keg Burning, like School Climbing. It took numerous calls from Mr. Montana and a great deal of reasoning to keep Maxwell's Harvard career alive.

Chas, on the other hand (oh, poor Chas) had the drive that Mr. Montana had hoped would go to Maxwell . . .

Or rather, Chas had the desire for *money* that Mr. Montana had hoped would go to his more intelligent son.

Chas, however, would not have made it into Harvard if not for his father's standing with the school—both as an alum, and as a premier donator. Chas was not intelligent enough. He lacked the proper sociopolitical acumen. He would never have stood on any sort of pedestal without a boost from his father.

For instance: Chas was president of the Harvard University Boxing Club during his final two years at the school. He felt great about this achievement. He felt proud. He never found out that Mr. Montana had pulled an entire network of strings to secure him that position.

Mr. Montana did not do this for his son, of course. He did it for himself.

After Chas graduated, he began working for his father. He worked in order to earn two things: Money and Approval, but he never could quite do enough to earn a satisfactory amount of either.

Maxwell, on the other hand... well, Maxwell worked for nothing, because he didn't actually work. Instead, he took the small allowance his father gave him, and he made the most of it. He maximized. He lived life.

Then, there was Jez—the brilliant, good-looking, hard-working young man who rose from nothing to his position within Montana Inc. because of his drive, charisma, and appealing personality.

As far as Mr. Montana could understand it, Chas and Maxwell were failures.

Jez was the perfect employee.

Jez was the perfect son.

* * *

Not long after Maxwell pulled me outside and talked to me about Lenore and Jez, I had an opportunity to speak with the latter, alone, for the first time. As with many of the things that occurred during those early days that launched this story, that conversation was unsuspectingly monumental. That conversation sparked our tenuous friendship. Neither of us envisioned or even imagined, at the time, the manner in which this friendship would end.

"Hello, Richard."

I looked over my shoulder at Jez standing in the corner of the porch—he had slipped outside without me noticing. "Jez, hey." I began to stand.

"Keep your seat there, friend. You mind if I join you?"

"No. Go ahead."

He sat beside me and crossed his legs in the way women or artists or successful men cross their legs. He folded his hands on his lap. "Where did Maxwell disappear to?" he asked.

"Oh, he—I think he went to the bathroom. That was a while ago, though. He may have gotten sidetracked."

"That tends to happen to him."

"Well—"

"I apologize for that conversation in there."

"Excuse me?"

Jez continued to watch the ocean the way a king might watch his kingdom. "Back in there, with Mr. Montana. I could tell that you were growing a bit bored—it's all rather dull at times, listening to him talk. It's insightful, mind you—you can sure learn a lot. But it's all rather dull at times. I tried to change the subject for you, but it seems that I was egregiously unsuccessful."

"I didn't mind so much."

"So, you're a writer, huh?"

"Huh? Oh—yes, that's right."

"I've read your book, you know."

"Have you?"

"You're quite talented, Richard. It was one of the more enjoyable books I've read. You have a nice grasp of the tone of a story. You know that? You have a nice understanding of people."

"Thanks. Do . . . you read a lot?"

"I do. Not as much as I would like to, of course. I read whenever I have the opportunity, but my time is quite constrained between work and more work."

"No wife, I guess."

"Not yet."

"No girlfriend?"

Jez smiled at me. His smile was perfect—but not perfect in that way that makes you hate someone. He looked endlessly astute and sincere and likable. "Not now," he said.

I returned his smile.

Maxwell returned outside not long after that, and he stood at the end of the porch and smoked a cigarette and kept reaching up with both his hands to push his hair off his face. None of us spoke after that, but it was not a strained silence. It was the silence of a beautiful day.

Mamma Montana poked her head outside several minutes or hours later.

"Boys, it's time for the meal. Come on inside now."

The table was set in the way rich people set their table for important, informal get-togethers: china that should probably have been on display rather than on the table, silverware that a burglar might steal, ornate wine glasses, napkins you couldn't use, and a tablecloth that made you afraid to eat lest you spill some food off your plate.

Mr. Montana said a quick, soulless grace, and Mamma Montana picked up her fork and poked around at her food and jumped right into Mamma character:

"Richard, dear, tell us what you're thankful for."

Maxwell dropped his knife onto his plate. "Aw, come on, Ma—don't do that to him."

"Quiet, Maxwell. It's Thanksgiving, in *case* you didn't notice."

"It's Tha—it's Thanks*giving*? Well shit, Ma, I *didn't* notice."

"Maxwell—"

"Mamma," Cecilia said, "he's only horsing around."

"I don't care what he's doing, I don't like that kind of language at the table. I'm sorry, Richard. Please forgive my son's manners."

Cecilia punched my leg under the table. I looked at her. Her mouth was scrunched in barely-contained laughter.

"You can leave if you want to," Maxwell said to me. He was eating mashed potatoes with his fingers. "I'm sorry to've embarrassed you with such *vul*gar language, I know you're not used to it. Why, it wouldn't surprise me if you didn't ever want to see us again."

Mr. Montana said Maxwell's name.

Maxwell winked at me, then he returned to his plate.

"So sorry, dear," Mamma Montana said. "You were saying?"

"Oh. I, um . . . "

"Here, Mamma," Cecilia said. "How 'bout if I go first."

"Oh yes. Wonderful, dear."

We all watched Cecilia.

I watched Cecilia. I certainly didn't mind.

Cecilia was absolutely lovely—that was the only way to describe her.

Her eyes spoke with the same sort of passion as her lips, glowing green and beautiful, with long eyelashes and impeccable shape.

Her hair was red. Gorgeous. Her hair would have touched her shoulders if it weren't pulled up in a ponytail, but a ponytail (loose and messy, with wisps of hair tracing the edges of her forehead so that she was always reaching up and pushing them out of her eyes) shaped her face more perfectly than any other style, and damn if she wasn't aware of all that.

Her lips were soft, and they softly said words that I hardly even heard.

Several minutes flew by before her words stopped singing.

Mamma Montana applauded.

"I'm thankful that I have such a perfect daughter like *you*," she said. She showed every one of her teeth, and Cecilia did the same.

Somewhere, a clock ticked. Somewhere, time disappeared.

Somewhere, Maxwell laughed.

"Oh, come off it," Mamma Montana said. "Just because you haven't got a heart doesn't mean the rest of us can't have one. I swear," she said to me, "Maxwell could freeze the wax off a candle—the boy hasn't got any heart at all."

Cecilia punched me under the table.

After dinner we played a board game I had never seen before (Mamma Montana's idea) and—like most board games—it was confusing and mildly pointless.

Maxwell made irreverent comments throughout most of the game.

Chas did his best to lose so that he could leave and go anywhere else.

"If L*enore* was here, you'd be more fun," Mamma Montana kept saying to Chas. "I sure wish L*enore* was here!"

Mr. Montana refused to play, and he poured a drink for himself and told us he would be in the library doing some research and not to disturb him unless it was an emergency.

Cecilia trash-talked Mamma Montana and laughed at herself every time she messed something up.

Jez looked stoic. He looked serene. He nearly managed to look as if playing this board game pleased him, but he couldn't quite pull it off.

After the board game ended, Cecilia helped Mamma Montana with the dishes while Maxwell gave me a tour of all three overlarge floors of the house. When we came back downstairs, Cecilia took my hand and led me outside.

I enjoyed Cecilia. She was pleasant to be around. She was pretty to look at and she wasn't dumb, so she was pleasant to be around.

She and I spent most of that evening together. We walked along the shore. We sat on rocks and talked. We moved to Banucci Manor and sat across from one another in the sitting room upstairs.

Outside the glass doors, the night was cold.

"I've read *A Dark Night in Rome*," Cecilia said.

"Have you?"

"I have." She chuckled. "Have you ever noticed how much of conversation is nothing but empty words?"

"Huh? I—"

"I mean . . . like, I told you that I've read your book. And you said, 'Have you?' And it's like, of course I have. Right? I mean, I just *said* that."

"Oh. I'm sorry."

"No. *No*, don't say sorry!" She reached forward and touched my knee. "I wasn't saying *you*. Like, I wasn't saying what you just said was . . . well, not *on*ly what you just said. Was empty words. But just that conversation, *all* conversation, in general, really has so many statements programmed into it that do nothing but fill the air. And people need that, they really do. But it's funny, ya know? Why can't people just talk, right? Without needing confirmation that the other person agrees, or that the other person is listening. I don't know. Ya know?"

"I know what you mean."

"Anyhow, sorry if I offended you."

"Oh! You didn't offe—"

"Anyhow, I was saying that I read your book."

"Right."

"Right, yeah. I *real*ly liked it. A *lot*."

"Thank you."

"I just loved how much depth the characters had. Do you know what I mean? I . . . well, the way I describe it to my friends is—when I closed the book, it didn't feel like I'd finished reading a book. It felt like I was saying good-bye to real-life *people*."

"Thank you. That's really nice."

"I think Max was mortified yesterday, after he mentioned you—after he said something about you staying here all alone. Mamma just *flipped* out. She was like, 'Oh, we *can't* let the poor boy stay all by himself over there. We *have* to invite him over for Thanksgiving.' Maxwell was *mort*ified. I was ecstatic, though. I don't even think Mamma knew who you were—*knows* who you are, even. Dad knows, he read your book. Jez and Chas, too.

Mamma's one of those women who reads nothing but self-help books. Ya know?"

"Yeah," I said. I chuckled. "I know."

"There it is again!"—her smile: Radiant. "Like, why did I ask you 'ya know?' Ya know? That was totally and completely *point*less."

"Yeah. I don't mind."

"I don't mind either."

We looked at each other.

Silence lingered.

"I feel like I need a map," she said. "When I look in your eyes. I'm afraid I'll get lost."

We both smiled again.

Later that night Cecilia left and Maxwell came by. He rambled on about Lenore and about other things, and he talked about his family, and he told some story about Jez that I think was supposed to be derogatory, but I couldn't really understand him. I think that he probably was stoned, and he asked me if I had seen the picture of Lenore that his family had on the bookshelf in the drawing room.

I told Maxwell that I had not seen the picture.

I said: Hey, you sure talk about Lenore a lot.

Maxwell laughed and tossed his cigarette aside. "Yeah. She's my brother's wife, you know. She's like family."

"All right."

"She is. I mean, that's the only reason I'm talking about her. Chill out, Rich," and he sort of half-laughed.

After that, he left. I went inside and poured another drink. I opened my computer and tried to start writing.

Nothing came to me.

I typed the first stanza of Poe's poem, *The Raven*.

> *Once upon a midnight drearu, while I pondered, weak and weary,*

Over many a quaint and curious volume of forgotten lore—
While I nodded, nearly napping, suddenly there came a tapping,
As of some one gently rapping, rapping at my chamber door.
"'Tis some visitor," I muttered, "tapping at my chamber door—
Only this and nothing more."

I read it.
I noticed that I had misspelled "dreary."
I deleted the whole thing.
I stared at the blank screen, and I started over again.

* * *

"So, Richard," Mamma Montana said as she dropped burnt pancakes onto my plate. "Tell me—what do you do for a living?"

Cecilia leaned in close to me. "In case you can't tell, Thanksgiving is the only time of year when Mamma ever cooks." Both of us laughed.

"What's that, sweetheart?"

"Nothing, Mamma. Are there any rolls left from yesterday?"

"Check in the fridge."

"Richard is a writer," Cecilia said. She stood from her barstool.

"A *writer*. How *thrilling*. What do you write?"

"I, uh . . ."

"He writes fiction, Mamma. Novels."

"Let Richard tell me, dear."

"The pancakes, Mamma. They're burning."

"Oh! Oh, dammit!"

Later in the day—

"You an investing man, son?"

The ladies had left for the 11:00 a.m. ferry so they could drive to Boston and shop, and Maxwell had disappeared, and I was stuck in the drawing room with the men. Crowded around the coffee table. Drinks in hand.

"I pay attention to the market," I said. "My dad was a financial advisor."

"What firm is he with?" Chas asked.

"Oh. Well, um. He's not with anyone, anymore. He passed away a few years ago."

"*My* dad was an options man," Mr. Montana said.

"I'm sorry about that," Chas said. "How did he die?"

"How did *who* die?" Mr. Montana asked. "This boy," he said to me, "he gets off on the most irrelevant tangents. Like I was saying, though, my father traded options. I tend to think that options aren't a sure enough bet, if you know what I'm saying. Even if you *don't* know what I'm saying, really." He chuckled to himself. He looked at me. "I'm sure your dad would agree with me. You say he's a financial advisor?"

"Was," I said. "He passed away a few years ago."

"I'm sorry to hear that, son. My dad passed away a few years ago as well. I know, it sure isn't easy. Looks like you came out of it all right, though. Didn't you."

"Yeah. Yessir, sure I did."

"Sure you did. But like I was saying..."

Maxwell was absent for most of the time while the women were away, and to tell you the God's honest, I'm not sure where he disappeared to.

If I had to guess, I would tell you that he probably sneaked over to the library at Banucci Manor, and he probably smoked a joint (joints?) and drank scotch while he browsed through books. He probably read aloud to himself and sank beneath the words, and sank beneath the world.

Wherever he went, I missed him. That day and a half without the women dragged on for eons, and the only respite in my life during this span was Jez and the knowledge that he was sympathetic toward my plight. Sometimes he gave me a knowing smile while Mr. Montana talked and talked. Sometimes he and I escaped together, and we chatted about things not doing with money or investing.

I came to know Jez better—at least, I came to know his impenetrable outer shell better, which was as well as Jez allowed most people to know him at all.

I realized early on in my interaction with him that he was a quality man.

I like that phrase, *A Quality Man*, and even though I'm not certain what it means, exactly, I use it for Jez because . . . because that's what he was. He was the kind of man you would take home to your sister. The kind of man you would trust with every one of your secrets. The kind of man, it seemed, who would never do a thing to cross you.

In the bubble that absorbed us during our time without the women—as I somehow became trapped in this cyclical conversation that explored nothing of real life—Jez was my anchor.

I came to like him a lot.

Having said all that . . .

I swear to you, by the time the women returned, if I had to hear the word 'stock,' 'option,' 'sector,' or 'hedge' one more damn time . . .

"Richard!"

"Hi, Cecilia. How was your shoppi—whoa!" She jumped into my body, and I caught her in my arms. We twirled in a circle as Mamma Montana watched us from beside the car and smiled.

"Oooh, you're pretty good at that!" Cecilia said.

I set her down in the grass. "I practiced with Maxwell while you were away."

"Silly! How was your time with the men?"

"My time with the men?" I gave Cecilia a look that said, 'Come on, are you kidding?'

Cecilia laughed out loud. "That's what I figured," she said, still laughing. "Wait'll you see the stuff I bought. We did *great*."

"You look like it."

"Hi, Richard—how was your time with the boys?"

"Excellent, Mamma Montana. How was shopping?"

"Would you be a dear and help me with these bags?"

"Sure," I said. I helped her with the bags.

The rest of the men were still inside.

That evening, we all ate dinner together, and that night I wandered off with Cecilia.

Cecilia and I sat in leather recliners on the roofed terrace outside the second-floor sitting room of Banucci Manor, and we were discussing the Jazz Age when she reached for my hand.

"It's such a gorgeous night," she said. "Don't you agree?"

Her fingers played across my knuckles.

"Is that one of those things," I said, "like you were saying the other day?"

"Huh?"

"Like, if I answer that, would it be just empty words? Plugging the holes of silence?"

"No!" she said, laughing. "Well...maybe." She looked beautiful. "Sorry."

"I don't mind."

"I don't mind either."

Silence.

I leaned over the empty space between the two recliners, and her fingers tightened against the back of my hand. Our lips pressed together.

She stood from her chair and climbed on my lap, and she and I kept kissing.

Outside the terrace, rain began to fall.

* * *

The next morning, Cecilia woke me with a knock on the study window. I had fallen asleep, again, in the chair at the desk.

"Good morning, handsome."

" 'Morning." I ushered her inside. We didn't kiss. We didn't hug. We barely made eye contact. I said, "How did you sleep last night?"

"On my side."

"On your . . . ? Oh!" I chuckled. "On your side. *Touché.*"

"How did you sleep?"

"Sitting up. And not too pleasantly."

"Why do you do that?" she said. I watched her drift across the room, and her hand trailed along the top of the couch, and she seemed, in general, to be not-quite-fully-there-with-me.

"Do what?" I said.

She made her way to the window and looked through it at the dancing eternity of grass and ocean and sky. "Fall asleep sitting up like that?" she said. "It seems *wild*ly uncomfortable."

"It is uncomfortable. Believe me. But . . . it just sort of happens sometimes."

"A *lot* of times."

"No. Not a lot of times."

"Well. The last two nights, at least."

"True. The last two nights." I walked over to the window and stood beside her, and we watched the world together.

That morning the temperature rose above fifty—unseasonably warm. I made coffee, and Cecilia and I began to become more comfortable, and we strolled down the shore.

Eventually we found a spot along the lace fringe of the water and settled down together. Cecilia kicked off her shoes. The water touched her toes.

"Isn't that cold?"

"I don't know," she said, quietly, thinking. "I've never thought of it before." She stuck one foot all the way forward, and the water washed over it. "Don't you just a*dore* the ocean?"

"I do," I said. I said this because there wasn't a whole lot else to say.

"I just love how big it is. How *grand*. I love how tiny we look compared to it. Don't you, Richard?"

"Yeah. Sure."

"Smile, why dontcha!" Cecilia grabbed my arm and leaned against me.

I smiled at the ocean. I smiled at her.

A couple hours later, the Montanas left.

Cecilia stood on tiptoes in the driveway and kissed me on the cheek.

Maxwell had just walked outside.

"Aw, c'mon, man! Save it for the bedroom."

"Shut *up*, Max!" Cecilia said. She laughed, and drops of sunshine dripped onto her face.

Mr. Montana stepped outside and shook my hand, and Chas did the same. Said good-bye.

Jez shook my hand and hugged me.

Mamma Montana gave me a big hug, and Maxwell gave me a bigger one. "If you get a break from your writing, brother, how 'bout if you give me a call—we'll have a good time in the city."

Cecilia pushed him aside, and she hugged me again, then she pulled away and they all began to leave.

The six of them traveled in two separate cars, heading to the mainland where they would go their separate ways—Maxwell and Chas would go to Boston, where Maxwell lived and where

Chas lived near, and the other car would meander down to Providence, where Jez and Cecilia lived and where Mr. and Mamma Montana lived near. Both cars were nearly to the large, iron, ivy-covered gate that marked the front of their garish kingdom when the lead car stopped. The second car stopped behind it. Maxwell hopped out of the front seat of the front car and jogged until he reached me.

"I forgot to tell you," he said. He shoved his hair off his forehead. He rested his hands on my shoulders. "If you run out of alcohol over at Sandy's—or if you just need a larger selection—they have a key to our house in the drawer under the sink, 'kay?"

"Okay. Well, thanks. I don't think I'll—"

"No, no, seriously. What's ours is yours. Also, I have a small sack of grass in . . . in one of my dresser drawers. Not sure which one. If you want any . . . "

I thanked him again.

He hugged me again, then he jogged away. "Call me," he shouted. "See you sometime," he shouted. The cars disappeared through the gate, and I didn't see any of them for another two weeks.

I never touched the marijuana while the Montanas were away. I hardly touched their alcohol.

I did spend some time in The Palace, however. And at some point during this space of time alone on the island, I stumbled upon a puddle of Mystery. It was something so small, so seemingly insignificant, but—isn't that always the way it goes?—it was this inconsequential burst of intrigue that set me on the path I followed for the next several weeks. This cracked door, which opened into a room I should probably never have entered.

* * *

The letter was written in a thin, sloping, handsome manner—the penmanship of an aged gentleman who likely fit the description of *an aged gentleman* in every fine sense of the term.

> *Dearest Lenore,*
>
> *I hate to receive such sad discourse from you. I read your letter over breakfast this morning, and it hurt my heart to imagine you in such a state.*
>
> *I wish that I could speak to you directly, but alas——*

I folded the letter and held it in fingers that were squeezing more tightly than they needed to be squeezing.

I had been exploring when I found this letter—I don't know what I was looking for, exactly. Perhaps I was looking for something exactly like this.

When you're a writer, and you cannot write, you wander. Without always realizing it inside your conscious mind, you search for a spark for a story.

A family like the Montanas—so spoiled and affluent and overflowing with the possibility of fascinating adventure—who knew what I might find? Who knew what secrets they hid?

I kicked around in closets in their home. I lifted dust ruffles and bent over and glanced under beds. I opened bathroom cabinets. I explored.

I sought no treasures. I intended no harm.

I was merely a ghost who wandered through a world in which he existed but did not belong.

I found the letter in an old, hardcover copy of John Steinbeck's *East of Eden*, in a drawer in the table beside Chas and Lenore's bed.

I opened the letter, and I read only just so far and stopped. I felt a pang in that part of the belly where Conscience holds court. This is wrong, it told me.

Yes.

I picked up the book and put the letter back inside.

I opened the book. I pulled the letter out. I unfolded the letter again, and I continued to read.

I wish that I could speak to you directly, but alas, pen and paper will have to suffice until I depart from the villa. I will call you as soon as I arrive back home, but please, my dear, advise me in your next letter whether I should depart forthwith. I know you would not desire to trouble me, so know that this is an honest and sincere invitation. Do you need me straightaway? If Yes, I will arrange to return to the city early, and I will arrange for you to meet me.

In the meantime, I have some thoughts that might lend strength to your tired soul, until such a time as I can see you and wipe the tears from your eyes with the tips of my fingers rather than simply with words. Please accept these morsels of wisdom from an old soul such as mine, however archaic they might seem to your vivacious and effervescent mind.

My primary advice to you is as follows: Time has a way of working out even the most insurmountable of problems.

I know this provides precious little solace to one currently mired in one such problem, so here is a bouquet of lifelines on which to cling until that time when the work of Time at last begins to show—

Lenore, you loved Chas once. I know this, because you told me. Remember this, because maybe you can love him still.

No man is perfect. No man is ever the man he wishes he could be, but the question is whether he wishes. The question is whether he strives.

I am certain he wants to do right, my dear. I am certain he truly loves you.

There was happiness, in that unseen past of yours. The key is figuring out how to uncover this happiness and return to where it began.

Have you spoken to him about this? Perhaps you should.

Perhaps you ought to talk to him about what you know, Lenore. Perhaps, also, you ought to be honest with him about what he does not yet know himself.

I am here for you, my love.

I await your response, and I look forward to seeing you in London at the end of November, if not sooner.

With love, always,

Grandpapa

P.S. Please give my greetings to young Mr. Tagsam, and tell him I think of him often.

CHAPTER 3

I sat in the chair at the desk in the study, sleeping, with a blank document open on the computer in front of me, and some sort of pounding invaded my dream, and then I startled awake and the pounding pervaded the real world as well. Someone was knocking on the door.

"Richard! Richard, are you there?"

A woman's voice.

The knocking.

"I'm coming..."

I pulled open the door.

Her hair was all astorm, and tears painted black streaks of makeup down the sides of her face.

"Mamma Montana! Come in."

She put her hands on my hips. She moved her hands to my back. She pulled my body toward her.

I hugged her—one of those awkward hugs, with our feet miles apart and our collarbones about the only parts of our bodies that touched at all. I had no clue what was happening.

In my ear, Mamma Montana cried.

"Shhh, shhh, it's okay. It's all okay, Mamma Montana. Don't cry."

She let go and stumbled past me into the sitting room where she collapsed on the couch. She smelled like she had soaked herself in gin.

I settled into the salmon-colored chair and looked outside at the morning.

The sun seemed to frown, puffing across the ocean and breathing through the window in sighs of cloud-covered light.

"Mamma," I whispered. "Mamma Montana." Somewhere, a clock ticked. Somewhere, time disappeared. From somewhere, far away, Mamma Montana looked up.

"I'm so sorry, dear. Darling. I'm so sorry for being this way."

"You're okay," I said. "It's all okay."

"She's dead," Mamma Montana said. "She's dead, Richard. We don't know what to do."

Mamma Montana continued to cry for a while.

I sat and watched and said nothing.

Finally, she stood. She left. I followed her. We walked through the grass together to the front door of The Palace.

"Good to see you, son. Thanks for coming over." Mr. Montana held out his hand. I gripped it tight. Looked him in his eyes. "You holding up all right?"

"I . . . yessir. Yes, I am. How about yourself?"

"I'll tell you, Chas sure is taking it tough. It's one of those things, you know? You never expect it to happen. You hear about these things, but they always feel as though they're so far away."

"Yessir. I know what you mean."

"It's life, son. It's an absolute puzzle. You couldn't figure it out if you tried. People *have* tried, believe me. That's the crazy thing. Why, I knew this young man in college, back during my Harvard days, mind you, and he was convinced—absolutely *convinced*, I tell you—that he would figure things out. All of this craziness that we call life. He used to say it all the time. You know what he would say?"

"No sir."

" 'I'm going to solve this damn puzzle that we call life. I promise you, Charles, I'm going to solve it.' That's what he would say. You know what happened to him?"

"No sir, I don't."

Mr. Montana put his two longest fingers against his temple. He held his thumb up like the hammer on a gun, and he pulled the hammer down. He made a gunshot noise. Something like this: *Phoom.*

I shook my head.

Mr. Montana shook his.

I found Chas in the drawing room, slumped over in one of the chairs in the semi-circle around the coffee table—his eyes open but unseeing. His body looked like a dead man's, propped up in a chair and forgotten. I stopped behind him and touched his shoulder.

"Oh," he said. He looked up and wiped his face. "Hello, Richard. How are you?"

I sat down beside him. "You doing all right?"

"Funny you should ask," he said. He stared at the sunlight on the bare wooden floor. The day looked so alive through the window. The day looked so opposite of everything inside. "To tell you the truth, I'm *not* doing so well."

"Hey, Chas." I waited for him to look at me, but he didn't. I continued. "Hey, you'll get through this. We're here for you, okay? It's all okay."

"Let's go over to Sandy's house," he said. "Let's go over there. I could sure use a drink. Could use a break."

"You sure?"

"I'm sure."

"Sure thing," I said.

We left.

In the early pages of this memoir, I touched upon the interpretive liberties that people—often strangers—tend to take with my personality and my Self, as if my reticence and contemplativeness provide for my social counterpart a sort of empty vessel, into which they may pour all the elements they desire me to have.

I was more than a little surprised when Chas solicited my participation in his monumental moment of mourning. As we crossed the grass, however, and said nothing and shared the day with the uncaring ocean, I began to understand.

Just as I had been for many people, many times before, I was to serve as a fill-in-the-blank for Chas. In this instance, I was a caring, compassionate friend. I was a writer, wise beyond my years. I understood what he was going through in a way that no one else could.

I poured a drink for him and made it strong. He was sitting in my chair—the salmon-colored chair by the window—and I handed him his drink and faced the couch for a moment before sitting. Neither of us spoke. He finished his drink, and I got up and poured him another.

"I wish you could've met Lenore," he said. He was leaned forward holding the glass on his knees with both hands. He spoke into the glass, and his words ran together.

"I know," I said. "I . . . I've heard nothing but good things about her, she . . . "

"She was great, man." He leaned back. He raised the glass to his lips. "Yeah, Richard. I wish you could've met her."

"You want me to pour you another drink?"

He looked down at the glass, as if surprised to find it empty. "Sure. Yeah, that'd be great."

As Chas worked his way through Glass Number Three, he began to open his thoughts. He opened them in the way a sober person might while alone when a particularly pensive mood strikes, moving through ponderous issues with reverent deliberation. Except, Chas was not alone. And he worked through his thoughts aloud, like a fisherman gutting a fish and flopping the guts onto a table for another to examine.

He talked about how, when you were with Lenore, you always felt like you were the only thing that mattered to her, like you were the single most important person in the world.

Lenore cared about people, he said, in a way you hardly ever see—she cared about each person as an absolute individual. Lenore could be around someone for a week, or less, and understand them in ways no one else ever had before.

Lenore touched something inside you, Chas told me. Everything about her, it was all so intangible, so indefinable. But when you met her, you understood. You knew you would never meet another person quite like her, no matter how long you lived.

I poured a fourth glass for Chas, and he told me a story about the time when he and Lenore spent the day at an amusement park in New Hampshire, and something about a child who had become separated from her parents, and something about Lenore, and something about how she was so great and he missed her so much—he continued to sip his whiskey, and the story progressively made less and less sense.

It didn't matter, I got the picture—Lenore was perfect, that's what Chas was saying. And she wasn't just perfect for him. Lenore was actually perfect.

I thought about what Maxwell had said, about Chas and his girlfriend Lily.

I thought about the letter I had found, in the book in their bedside table.

Chas continued talking and drinking, and soon he quit both at once and started snoring in the chair.

* * *

Jez and Cecilia arrived early the next morning. I met them at the front door of The Palace, and Cecilia gave me a hug while she tried to swallow her tears. "Isn't it awful, Richard?"

"It is."

"Richard," Jez said.

"Jez." We shook hands and hugged with our free arms. He patted my back a couple times before releasing me.

"How's Chas holding up?"

"Not so well," I told him.

Jez shook his head. "What a shame. Isn't it? A damn crying shame."

The three of us stepped inside, and at some point Cecilia pulled me outside again and we walked along the shoreline with our jackets pulled up around our necks, and we turned around after not too long and were inside again and I was sitting with Chas in the drawing room and he looked through the window on the verge of tears but no tears came to him, and Mamma Montana joined us at some point and Chas left and Mamma Montana and I continued to sit there together saying nothing, and everything in the day collided together in a melting stream of subdued emotions and conversations that accomplished absolutely nothing.

In the evening, Jez asked if I felt like slipping away from the family and going over to Banucci Manor for a spell. We sat on the terrace outside the second-floor sitting room, drinking whiskey and smoking.

The night passed us, and we watched the waves crash, and everything was still.

Jez and I examined different topics of interest to us both— literature, classical music, the state of America, horse racing. We laughed at times, but we laughed quietly—as if preserving the seriousness of the situation that had befallen the Montana family.

I leaned over and picked up the bottle of whiskey and poured another drink for myself. I lit a cigarette.

I asked Jez about Lenore—How well had he known her?

"That's a pretty subjective question." He picked up his glass. He took a sip. "How well did I know her? I guess you'd have to ask her."

"Geez. That's a bit insensitive."

"How's that?" He set the glass down.

"I mean, considering she just died and all. It's just . . . "

"I didn't mean anything by it, Richard—I didn't mean anything like that. I'm sorry."

"No, it's just—"

"I'm sorry. Apologies."

I never received an answer from Jez that night—How well had he known Lenore?—and looking back, I realize that he sidestepped the question. If I hadn't been drinking, I might have noticed. I might have given this appropriate attention.

As it was, Jez changed the subject and I followed along behind him.

Later that night Jez left Banucci Manor and walked with the erect carriage and leisurely gait of a successful sober man out for a stroll. His lonely figure cut an impressive picture as it ambled toward the enormity of The Palace.

It's comical.

It's sad.

But also, it's true: Tragedy brings people together.

When I awoke late the next morning, I walked through the cold, wet grass to The Palace, and I ate cereal and a toasted bagel while Jez and I sat together in the upstairs living room—watching the sunlight pour down on the ocean.

"What's the mood been like over here this morning?" I asked.

"Subdued. Sedated."

"It seems that way."

Jez shook his head and stared through the glass. "For good reason. Did you hear that Mr. Montana finally got a hold of the airline last night?"

"Nuh-uh. What did they say?"

"They checked the manifest. Told him that Lenore had definitely gotten on the flight."

"Geez. That's awful," I said.

Jez sipped his coffee. "It really is."

We continued to watch the day, and I imagined Lenore from the photograph downstairs. I pictured her pretty face—sure, she was pretty, but . . . what? But everyone said there was something else about her. Something intangible. Something you could only understand if you met her.

I pictured Lenore, dead.

I glanced at Jez. I wondered what he must be feeling.

Jez sipped his coffee, and we continued to watch the day.

"Where do you think Maxwell is?" I asked him.

He looked at me. He looked back out through the window. "No telling for sure. But I'd say somewhere. Drinking."

"That's what I figured. You think he knows yet?"

"About Lenore?"

I nodded.

"I'm sure he got the messages, yeah. I'm sure he knows by now."

"You don't think he'd be here by now, if he already knew?"

"I think that Maxwell will need some time alone," Jez said.

"Some time alone for what?"

"My friend." He paused. He looked at me. "That's a story you don't know the half of. I bet you will, though. In fact, I'm sure you will—I'm sure that Maxwell will tell you."

Jez and I left the living room, and we joined the nothing-going-on downstairs.

Those days after Lenore died and before she arrived alive on the island were a frenetic mishmash of words and movement. There were six of us in The Palace, but at times it seemed more like sixty, and at other times it seemed as if no one—not even myself—was inside that overlarge house, as if emotions skulked around on feet of their own, passing through rooms like vapor.

Conversations rose and merged and dwindled. Words that seemed important at the time were sucked away and forgotten the moment they hit the air. The days dragged on for ages, and they disappeared in a flash.

Each person dealt with the grief in their own independent way.

Mamma Montana buzzed from room to room, tidying up messes that never existed in the first place. She mumbled just under the surface of audibility about a memorial service. She dabbed at her eyes with theatrical gravity.

Mr. Montana mostly hid himself in the library. If you talked to him about anything, he changed the subject to something else. Sometimes, he left the library and strode importantly to the kitchen or the stairs only to turn around and retrace his steps. Each time he reentered the library, he closed the door softly.

Every time I saw Chas, he was holding a drink. He bestowed a benevolent smile upon any of us who looked at him, and the smile was so affected as to be painful for the receiver and, most likely, painful for Chas. We stopped looking at him, and he drifted through the house like an orange blob inside a lava lamp, with a cold glass of whiskey glued to his hands.

When Jez and I talked, he talked about tragedy and he talked about Lenore. He spoke philosophically, knowingly. He spoke with great grace, the way he always spoke. If not for his unmarred appearance—his beautiful face with skin so soft, and his features all so perfect—you might truly believe that he was possessor of an especially long and arduous life, and that he had been in this exact situation many times before, and that if you hung around him long enough you would likely find him in this exact situation sometime again.

Also, there was Cecilia.

I have often wondered, in these heavy days since my time on Nantucket, what I was thinking at the time.

Cecilia was a beautiful young lady, to be certain. She was a fun girl, and easy to be around, and easy to talk to.

But Cecilia . . .

You see, I grew up in Texas, just outside of Dallas. My father worked at a convenience store, and when my mother was seven months pregnant with me, the convenience store was robbed and my father was shot in the frenzy that followed. He died four days later, and my mother put me up for adoption before I was born.

I still saw my mother, growing up. She came on Saturdays, once a month. She took me to the zoo, or to the aquarium, or to the apartments where she scored her drugs. She killed herself on the eve of my eighth birthday—she died lying in bed beside an empty bottle of Drano.

My adoptive parents were Norma and Jerry Parkland—a middle-class white couple who lived in a middle-class white neighborhood, with middle-class white ideas and ideals and problems. They were in their early forties when they adopted me. They cared for me the same way they would have cared for a son of their own.

I adored my Mum and Dad. I loved them more than anything.

They died when I was seventeen years old. They were driving up from Shreveport, where they'd been staying with friends, and a truck driver fell asleep and hopped the median and hit my parents head-on.

Afterward, I lived with my Mum's sister and her husband. A new house. A new neighborhood. A new place where I didn't belong.

Growing up, that was the thing—I never really belonged. Even when I was just a kid, I understood this. Their world was not my world. Their friends were not my friends. The school I attended was not my school.

I spent my whole life as an outsider—always an accepted member of my surroundings, but always also with some sort of thin, gelatin-like layer encasing me and separating me from everyone else.

I sought circumstances that made me feel as if this barrier had melted. I took in friends who made me laugh, because laughing allowed me to escape my analytical insides. I took in friends who needed help, because helping someone put us in the same world together.

I took in women. Not in a womanizing way, but in a way of alliance.

Women have a power we often overlook—the power of influence. This might be the individual female's most potent, most terrible weapon. I understood this long before I possessed the words to define it, and so I spent much of my adolescence seeking the next pair of warm, slender arms that allowed me to feel at ease, that allowed me to feel as if I belonged in a world where I had no place.

I never intended to hurt anyone—especially, I never intended to hurt Cecilia.

I truly enjoyed her company during my first few days on Nantucket. She would be leaving soon—and hell, I was unable to write at the time—and she was beautiful and vibrant and pleasant.

I had no idea that she would be back on the island so soon, and in such an emotionally precarious position.

That night, Cecilia curled her body into mine, and the fire crackled—toasting the bottoms of our feet.

Cecilia was facing away from me. She said, "Richard, what are you thinking about?"

"How beautiful you are."

"Stop it. Seriously."

"Seriously. That's what I was thinking."

"Really?"

"Yes ma'am. How beautiful you are." I kissed Cecilia's earlobe.

"You're too sweet," she said.

"I try."

"You do a good job."

I moved from her earlobe to her neck. "How about you?" I said between kisses. "What are you thinking of?"

The mood in the room darkened. "I was thinking about Lenore," she said.

I stopped kissing her neck. "Yeah?"

"Yeah. It feels so weird."

"What does?"

"The fact that she's gone. I'm so used to having her around."

I started to say something, then I stopped. No words were strong enough to fill the serious space of that moment. I kissed her neck again, one single time, then I leaned away and sighed.

"You'd understand if you knew her," she said. "Like, seriously—I'm not exaggerating at all. Lenore was the most amazing woman you'd ever met. I promise you, if I could become half the person she was . . ."

After a while, Cecilia rolled over and wrapped her legs through mine. Her lips touched my eyelids. Her lips touched my lips.

We kissed, and we lost ourselves. We lost the world around us.

Everything became a tumult of passion and movement and skin.

The heat from the fire licked our feet, and our bodies pressed together. Our legs intertwined. I heard the fire crackle.

We fell asleep in front of the fire, holding each other close.

* * *

Knocking on the door.

Cecilia's warm body pressed against mine. Neither of us wearing clothes. My legs twisted tightly under hers.

The knocking.

My brain fought to function: Is that knocking? Is someone knocking on the door?

The fire was nothing more now than a family of dying embers. The blanket around us absorbed the warmth of our bodies, and I held Cecilia closer to keep the warmth from escaping.

Knocking.

Cecilia awoke. She looked toward the door.

"Baby?" she said.

"Mmmgh?"

"What's that?" she said. "Is that the door?"

I slipped out from under the protection of the blanket. The night was dark. I fumbled around for my jeans. I was still buttoning them when I fell against the back door, and I pressed my eyes to the glass.

I lunged toward the handle and ripped the door open.

"Maxwell!"

I heard Cecilia gasp—"*Maxwell?*"

Maxwell tumbled forward and collided with my body. I grabbed his arm and flung it over my shoulders.

His arm was cold and dead, like rubber. His body felt heavy. I kicked the door shut with the back of my foot and we stumbled toward the couch.

We passed Cecilia—she was still on the floor by the fireplace, looking surprised, with the blanket around her breasts. Stray wisps of hair hung in her eyes.

"Richard, brother. Thank you for your help." These were the words Maxwell said. Meant to say, at least. They plopped out of his mouth in a slurred and messy bundle.

I laid him down across the couch. I propped his head up with a pillow.

"Hey, Cee," he said. "Whaddaryou doing here?"

"Max. Are you okay?"

"Cecilia, go get a glass of ice for me, will you?"

"Max?"

"*Cecilia.*"

"Sorry," she said. She struggled to stand with the blanket wrapped around her, and she scurried from the room—her feet disappeared inside the blanket's tumbling folds.

"So cooold out there. So damn *cold.*"

"You're all right, Maxwell. You're all right, bud. Just close your eyes. There, there you go."

"So damn cold, man. Huh, Richard old boy. How 'bout it."

"How 'bout it," I said.

Cecilia slid the glass into my hand, and I handed it to Maxwell. I heard her pick her clothes up and slip from the room.

She returned. Her clothes in place.

Maxwell's mouth was filled with ice—eyes closed and breathing heavy.

"Baby," she said.

I didn't answer. I didn't really hear her.

"Baby." Her fingers rested on my arm. I reached up and touched them. "Is he okay, baby?"

"I think so."

Maxwell's face was pale.

"Should I make some tea for him? Or something?"

"Do you know where to find some?"

"I think so."

I looked at her. Her eyes were green and sharp and lovely. "Yeah. Yeah, I think you should."

She left the room again.

Maxwell drank the tea and I sat with him while he drank it to make sure he didn't spill it and burn himself. When the tea was nearly finished, he dropped the mug on the floor.

Cecilia helped me clean up and she made some more tea for Maxwell, then I walked her outside.

We stood on the back patio. She looked up into my eyes. "You're absolutely *sure*?" she said.

"Yeah, Cecilia. I think it's for the best."

"I don't... I don't just wanna *leave* him like this."

"I'm going to take care of him. Don't worry about him, okay? You need sleep. Besides, it isn't going to help you to sit around and watch him like this."

"Well. But I just—"

"He's *fine*. Trust me, okay?"

"Okay," she said. She thought about it. "Yeah, okay. He'll be fine."

"He'll be fine," I echoed.

I kissed her good-bye.

Cecilia took about ten steps, then she stopped and turned around. The moon shone through a cloud, and her face looked solemn and wonderful. Her lips danced like a pair of goddesses. She waited for my reply.

"What's that?"

"I said: He'll be fine. Right?"

"Yeah," I said. I nodded. "Yeah, Cecilia. He'll be fine. I'll bring him over in the morning, good as new."

"Okay, baby. I'll see you then."

"See you then."

She blew me a kiss and faded across the lawn.

"Did you *bang* my lilll sister? Ha!—you *did*, didn' you? You sly little... fox. You."

"Drink your tea, Maxwell."

"Drink your tea, Maxwell. What am I, imcontpetent, or somethin'? C'mon, brother. *Look* at me! I'm fiiine."

"I'm sure you are," I said. I sat in the salmon-colored chair. "But I still think you ought to drink your tea."

"*Ought* to. That's better. Let's have some *respect* here. Whoa!" He caught himself from falling off the couch. "Almost had a spill there."

"Where have you been, Maxwell?"

"Ought to drink the tea. *Ought* to drink the tea. Tea-tea-teeeeeeea!" He took a big sip. Half of it missed his mouth and ran down his neck.

"Maxwell."

He looked in my general direction.

"Where have you been, huh?"

He shook his head. "Life's a bitch, brother." He shook his head harder. "An absolute bitch."

He closed his eyes and slept.

Four hours later:

Maxwell rolled over and searched the room until he figured out where he was, and he found me, and he stopped.

"Richard. How are you, brother?"

"How are *you*?"

"What day is it?"

"Saturday," I said.

"Saturday what?"

"December 13."

"Saturday. December 13." He rolled on his back and stared at the ceiling. "What time?"

"Five."

"A.m.?"

"A.m."

"Man." He looked at me again. "I was *out* of it last night."

"Yeah," I said.

"Yup. Man. Hey, can you get me a glass of water?"

"Sure thing. Ice?"

"Yeah."

"Sure thing." I closed my book (*Ulysses*, by James Joyce) and found my way to the kitchen.

Maxwell and I moved to the covered porch on the second floor, and we sat down and watched the ocean. He smoked a joint and guzzled cold water.

He told me about Lenore.

* * *

Baseball is the Great Bostonian Equalizer: Poor and Rich, Black and White, Young and Old—everyone breathes the Red Sox.

This is no joke. The daily mood of the city rides the wave of the previous night's outcome, and if the winter weather in Boston is bleak, it's nothing compared to the cloud that hung over the city for 86 years.

In 2004, however, an incredible thing happened: Ages of misery and bad luck ended in a screaming wave of success, and for the first time since 1918, the Red Sox were World Series champions.

The euphoria!

The love!

For a single night the whole city was family, bonded together through triumph. The mountain called Glory had at last been conquered.

If you've never lived in Boston, you can't possibly understand.

For a Bostonian there could be no better story than to someday say to your kids, "Have I ever told you how your mom and I met? I haven't? Well, it was October 27, 2004, and the Red Sox had won the World Series ... "

For Maxwell, however, there was no worse story than the way things ended up.

"Of *course*," he told me, sucking down his joint, "I was drunk."

"Of course."

He released the smoke from his lungs. Opened his eyes wide. Scratched his arm. "I left the bar, and I ran out into the street. Everyone was going wild. I mean, *wild*. You've never seen a damn thing like it."

Actually, I *had* seen a damn thing like it—had in fact seen *it* exactly.

Sandy and I drove up to Boston on the day of Game 4 and watched the game with some of his buddies in a bar near the ballpark. The game was being performed on a stage about 2,000 miles away, in balmy St. Louis—in the middle of nowhere as far as Boston was concerned—but fans all over the city crowded into restaurants and sports bars as close to Fenway as possible, and the Kenmore Square area morphed into a smorgasbord of drunken and passionate revelry. Everywhere you looked, there was red and navy blue. The letter 'B' was ubiquitous. Everywhere, everywhere: noise noise noise.

I sat there with Sandy and Sandy's buddies and watched the game and thought: This is what I love. This camaraderie and community, birthed from the womb of a single shared passion.

I was right there in the middle of the city, and Maxwell was somewhere nearby.

"I'm not even too big a fan, right? You know me—it's tough for me to be all real passionate about . . . about something. Or whatever. You know what I mean. But *hell*. Richard, brother, you couldn't *help* but get caught up in the excitement. The goddamn stripped-down pomp of it all—the whole city was high off the buzz. And they *won*, man—first time in 86 years. I sprinted into the street, ripped my shirt off and whipped it around my head. A couple of my buddies shimmied up these, um, these . . . street lights. One of them fell off, even. I didn't even see it. I was too goddamn busy sprinting around the street half-naked, yelling like a maniac. Of course, that's when I saw her."

She was in the street also, he said—not half-naked, not yelling. She wore a red Ted Williams T-shirt jersey and she had loose, black curls of hair that tumbled out from beneath an authentic Red Sox game hat. She smiled at one of her friends, yelled something to them, and her lovely British accent carried over the noise. In her hand she held a Coca-Cola. Under her T-shirt jersey she wore a thick, white hooded sweatshirt.

Maxwell straightened his drunken gait and walked toward her slowly. His mind moved fast. He tried to dig beneath the layers of alcohol, tried to uncover some sort of sane and sober greeting.

He smiled.

She smiled.

His feet carried him closer.

She leaned forward—hands in her pockets, shoulders shrugged up around her neck. "You look frigid," she said.

Maxwell kept walking, trying not to stumble.

"What's that?"

"I said you look frigid."

He laughed. He stepped onto the curb and stopped in front of her. He leaned away and looked down.

"What are you doing?" she said. She laughed. Her laugh was full and melodic.

"How tall are you?" he asked.

"That's the first real thing I ever said to her," he said to me, while we sat on the second-floor terrace and watched the sun peek up through the water. "Man was I drunk."

"I'm five-foot-ten," she said. "Shouldn't you be wearing a shirt or something?"

"I don't know where my shirt is."

"You're holding it."

"Huh?"

"In your hand. Right there."

"Oh," he said. "I am."

He lunged forward and kissed her.

* * *

"You *what*?"

"Kissed her."

"Just like that?"

"Brother, just like that."

I shook my head. "What a moron."

"Exactly," he said. "What a moron."

His joint was gone now—all smoked away. Both of us held a glass of scotch. The sun was less than halfway out of the water.

"How did she react?" I asked him.

"Not too well."

"*Excuse* me!" she said to him, and she shoved him away.

"What?" he said. He held his hands out in front of him like he didn't know what he'd done wrong.

Lenore shook her head. She turned and glided off.

"That's it?" I asked.

"It would have been."

"Would have been?"

"Would have been . . . "

He stopped. We sat in musical silence, listening to nature.

Fifty yards away, the water rushed up onto the sand. Somewhere, a bird sang. The wind blew in our faces, and I pulled my sweatshirt tighter.

"I followed her."

"Stop it."

"No kidding," he said. He reached into his pocket and retrieved his cigarettes. He knocked one out of the pack, then he fetched his lighter. "Yeah," Maxwell said, smoke issuing from his mouth. He offered me a cigarette with a twist of his hand. I waved him away. "Yeah, I followed her. All the way through the Back Bay."

We reached for our glasses at the same time. We each took a sip. Maxwell kept talking.

* * *

Lenore followed her friends into a dark and lively tavern. They sat at a booth in the corner, by the window. Outside the window, people passed.

Maxwell sneaked in and sat at the bar.

"What'll it be foyah," the bartender asked.

"Huh?"

"What'll it *be*? Yah gonna drink or yah just gonnah sit theh?"

"I..."

"I, I, come-awn, sistah, what'll it be?"

Maxwell ordered a beer. Lenore and her friends were singing:

Tessieeee, 'Nuff Said McGreevy shouted,
We're not here to mess around!
Boston, you know we looove you madly
Hear the crowd roar, to your sound ...
Don't blame us if we ever doubt you,
You know we couldn't live without you!
Red Sox! You are the only, only, ooooonly

They fell over each other in drunkenness. Only Lenore looked sober.

"Another round!" one of them yelled. The rest continued singing.

"Straws up!" another yelled. The rest of them were singing.

The other three passed their straws to Lenore, and she held them, and they picked. They all were still singing.

"This round on Lenore!" one of them yelled.

She held up the short straw.

"This round on me." She pushed herself out of the booth and walked (floated) to the bar.

"Four more," she called to the bartender.

"All right, sweethaht, give me just one second."

"Certainly," she said.

"Hey," Maxwell said. "Hey. *Hey!*"

She looked at him. Their eyes met.

She smiled and shook her head.

"Look, I—"

"It's okay," Lenore said. "Don't worry about it."

"Seriously, I—"

"Not a big deal."

"You sure?"

"I'm positive."

"All right, little lady," the bartender said, "theh're makin' you buy thah drinks again, huh?"

"I keep getting the short straw," she said. She laughed.

"It's a conspirahcy," he said.

She laughed again.

He pushed the drinks forward and she handed him the money.

"Keep it," she told him.

"How 'bout that."

"Here," Maxwell yelled, "here, I'll help you with those."

Lenore shrugged and picked up two mugs. Maxwell picked up the others.

They were halfway to the table when Maxwell tripped. He hit the ground and the mugs shattered. Beer sprayed everywhere.

* * *

Maxwell called it the most embarrassing moment of his life, and he probably was right.

But oh, Maxwell—you opportunistic bastard . . .

He apologized profusely and helped clean up and bought Lenore and her friends another round, then he asked the bartender for a pen. He wrote a note on a napkin. He handed the note to Lenore:

> *Seriously, I am so sorry for embarrassing you (and for embarrassing myself). No excuses. I would like to apologize properly. If you'll let me, meet me for dinner at A_____ P____ on Monday (November 1) at 7:30 P.M.*
>
> *Cheers.*
> *~ Maxwell Montana.*

"And . . . she showed up?"

"She did."

"Maxwell, that's pretty smooth."

He laughed. "Yeah," he said. He looked down. Sipped his scotch. "I was gonna just put down my number, but I figured she would never call me. But if she knew I was gonna be sitting at that restaurant all by my damn self . . . "

"Nice."

"It *was* nice. At first . . . "

At first . . .

It turned out that Lenore was a Harvard student also.

It turned out that she and Maxwell enjoyed the same authors. They enjoyed the same artists.

It turned out that the only music either of them ever listened to was nothing but The Beatles. Only The Beatles. Always The Beatles.

It turned out that Maxwell got along with Lenore better than he had gotten along with anybody in his whole entire life.

"I remember our first kiss . . . our first *real* kiss," he said. His eyes were closed. The ocean rose and fell, rose and fell, shining in the sun. "She and I were sitting on the roof, at my old apartment in Cambridge. It was November—late November—and we were sitting up there and I'd made a couple of grilled cheese sandwiches. We, uh . . . we had this blanket over us. We were sitting in different chairs, you know. In different . . . um . . . lawn chairs. But we were sharing this blanket. It was cold, I remember that, and both of us were shivering while we ate our sandwiches, and both of us talked and were laughing. There, um, there wasn't any sort of, like, segue, or anything. Into our kiss. But there was just this gap in our conversation, where everything went quiet. And we looked at each other. Right in the eyes. And that's when we kissed."

The kiss was like magic.

The kiss was the most real thing Maxwell had experienced in his whole entire life.

A month and a half later he introduced her to his family, and that's when Lenore met Chas—

"What!"

"Yup."

"You're kidding, Maxwell."

"Not kidding. I *wish* I was, brother. But seriously, not kidding."

December 31, 2004:

For the first time in forever, Maxwell attended the New Year's Eve party that his parents threw every year at The Palace.

It was the first time in his entire life that he had actually wanted to go.

He wanted to show Lenore off to his family. He wanted to show her off to their friends.

And show her off he did, and everyone was impressed. But when they asked Maxwell, this is what he said: "No, *no!*—Lenore and I are just friends."

"Really?"

"Yeah. Nothing more than friends." He said all of this with Lenore standing beside him, hanging off his arm.

Chas asked him, "You're serious?"

"Totally, brother. She and I are just friends."

"Wow," Chas said.

"Wow what?"

"Wow nothing. Just . . . wow."

When Cecilia asked him the same question, he told her the same damn thing.

Why?

He doesn't have a clue.

Even all these years later, Maxwell is convinced that he and Lenore would have dated—would probably have married, even—had he taken a different approach. Had he been honest and told his brother, "Well, we're not officially dating, but I do like her a lot."

The choices you make now will affect your whole life, and instead of telling Chas that he liked Lenore, he said that he wasn't interested in her at all.

The party ended and life continued.

Soon, Chas took Lenore on a date.

Soon, Chas and Lenore were in a relationship.

Soon, they were engaged.

They were married.

Maxwell was the best man in the wedding.

* * *

It is nothing to brag about, but whenever Maxwell drinks a lot he manages to operate within standard social structures as if nothing is wrong with him at all. It takes a lot of practice to master this talent, and Maxwell has mastered it well.

It is nothing to brag about, but I have become pretty adept at it myself.

This particular morning was the commencement of my training.

We left Banucci Manor at 7:00 a.m. and strolled through the soft, wet grass. The morning air bit the rims of my ears and the ocean's throb provided rhythm for my feet.

We entered The Palace through the side door.

We wiped our feet off and slid into the kitchen.

"Maxwell!"

"Good morning, Ma." He kissed her on the cheek.

"And just where, exactly, have you—"

"You look absolutely *ra*diant this morning, Ma. You sleep well last night?"

"I—oh, well thank you, Maxwell. I slept okay. I . . . wait," she said. "Oh, you're not gonna pull *that* on me."

"Pull what, Ma?" He padded to the refrigerator and grabbed the milk.

"Where have you been the last few days, young man?"

"On a bender. Hey, do we have any *decent* cereal?"

"I'm being serious, Maxwell."

"So am I. All we have up here are Corn Flakes and *Cheerios*. Where's the sweet stuff, huh?"

"I mean, I'm being serious about asking where you've been."

"I was being serious about that, too, Ma." He smiled at her.

She shook her head. She looked older and more tired.

"Don't worry," he said, "I'm all sobered up now. Just needed to get it out of my system. Richard, have a seat, brother." He patted the barstool beside him.

"So," she said to Maxwell, quietly. "You know about Lenore?"

He poured his milk. I sat down beside him. "I do."

"You doing okay?"

"How are *you* doing?"

"Oh," she said. She pushed her hair off her face. "I'm doing all right, I guess. Well, not *too* well. It really came as a shock, you know."

"I know, Ma. I know."

Later that morning, I sat with Jez and tried to focus on our conversation, but I kept getting distracted, wondering if he could tell that I was really terribly drunk.

"Was I right?" he asked me.

My mind spiraled. I wondered why I didn't remember the question he had asked.

"Hey, Richard—you okay?"

"I think so," I said. "I think so. I might be."

"You don't look so hot."

"I don't feel so hot."

"Maybe you ought to lie down."

"No," I told him. "No, no, I'm absolutely fine. What's that you were saying?"

"I, um . . . oh—oh, I was asking if I was right, about Maxwell giving you the background of his history with Lenore."

"Ah. Oh, yeah. Yes, he did. He told me the whole thing."

"Crazy," he said. "Isn't it?"

"It is."

We didn't speak for a while. Probably, it seemed like a much longer span of emptiness than it truly, honestly was.

"You know," Jez finally said. All his fluid words climbed up over perfect teeth, and they slid out from between soft, seamless lips. "You never met Lenore. If you had, you would understand better. But let me tell you something about her. Lenore? If you had a chance—a legitimate chance—to be with her . . . to share your life with her . . . and you screwed that up? Well. To put it plainly, it's something for which you would never forgive yourself. Never. That's no exaggeration."

"She was that amazing, huh?"

"She was that amazing."

Silence.

Thinking.

The alcohol making me bold ...

"So ... what's the deal with Chas, then?"

"How do you mean?"

"Well. He has a girlfriend, right?"

Jez's face changed. Some of his muscles tightened. For the first time since I'd met him, I saw wrinkles that were not symmetrical, that were not placed in the perfect location for accentuating his flawless features.

"That's not something that really involves us," he said. Sharply.

"No. But I'm still curious. *That's* not gonna change. If Lenore was so amazing, why ... "

"Why did he take her for granted?"

"Yeah."

"Because Chas is an asshole," he said.

I sighed and shook my head.

"Chas is a royal asshole," he said.

We both shook our heads.

* * *

Cecilia and I lay on the bed together, our bodies entwined, the sheets wet with sweat. We breathed heavy.

We kissed a bit without speaking.

Cecilia rolled over and tossed her arms around me.

Both of us were exhausted.

Ten minutes later, she told me she ought to leave.

"You serious?"

"Yeah, baby. I sleep better in my own bed. And besides, I don't want my parents—my *dad*, really—getting all up in arms, finding out that we're, ya know ... sleeping together."

"Okay, well . . . "

I offered to walk her home.

"I'm fine—I can walk by myself."

"You sure?"

"Of course I'm sure. I'm inde*pen*dent."

I chuckled. "All right. All right, sure. You're amazing," I said. "*You're* amazing."

We dressed, and I kissed her good-bye, and I watched her walk home.

Just before Cecilia reached The Palace, the clouds began to open. The rain fell heavy. Droplets of water splashed off the patio and landed on my ankles.

I closed the door and turned off every light except the one beside the desk, and I pulled out my computer.

> *Ah, distinctly I remember it was in the bleak December,*
> *And each separate dying ember wrought its ghost upon the floor.*
> *Eagerly I wished the morrow;—vainly I had sought to borrow*
> *From my books surcease of sorrow—sorrow for the lost Lenore—*
> *For the rare and radiant maiden whom the angels name Lenore—*
> *Nameless here for evermore.*

I wrote it. Read it. Cursed Poe.

I deleted the second stanza of *The Raven*, and I stared at the blank screen again.

I stared at the blank screen.

I stared at the blank screen.

I stared at the blank screen.

Fell asleep.

> And the silken sad uncertain rustling of each purple curtain
>
> Thrilled me—filled me with fantastic terrors never felt before;
>
> So that now, to still the beating of my heart, I stood repeating:
>
> " 'Tis some visitor entreating entrance at my chamber door—
>
> Some late visitor entreating entrance at my chamber door;
>
> This it is and nothing more."

Nothing more. Nothing more.

Nameless here for evermore.

Tell me—tell me, I implore!

Quoth the Raven, "Nevermore."

I startled awake.

Some one tapping, tapping at my chamber door.

I strained my eyes to see through the window, and on the back patio, in the rain, stood the most beautiful woman I had ever seen.

Whom the angels name Lenore.

CHAPTER 4

I sat beside Lenore in front of the fire. She was wrapped in a blanket, and I stared at the window on the opposite wall. My heart throbbed in my chest, like a spasmodic extension of my unrestrained wonder.

To meet Lenore would have been fantastic enough.

To meet Lenore four days after her death—while I was drunk and dozed off and staying at a mansion on the shores of the Atlantic—was like waking up from a spectacular dream to discover that the dream was a nightmare compared to the wondrous qualities of reality.

"What are you thinking about?" she asked me.

The next day I would ask Maxwell this same question, and he would tell me that it's probably one of the emptiest questions in history.

Right now, Maxwell did not exist to me.

"I," I said. "I was thinking about . . ." I was thinking about Lenore. But I didn't want to say that. I was thinking about her eyes—my goodness, if you could *see* her eyes—a deep, dark, unfathomable blue. A blue that exuded a mysticism that left you hollow and exposed. I thought about Lenore's voice, her melodic

British accent fingering the scales of musical perfection as though the words themselves were worthy of front-page billing in a lovely London opera. I thought about her face, her high cheekbones and perfect jaw. Her sensuous lips. Her perfection.

"...nothing much, I [*cough*], I guess. Sorry [*cough*], sorry."

"You're okay, Richard. You catching a cold?"

"I, yeah." I looked away. "I might be."

"You shouldn't have gone out in the rain like that. Here, take some of the blanket."

"No, no. Thanks, Lenore, but I'm fi—"

"I *insist*."

I grabbed a corner of the blanket from her outstretched hand. I placed it over my feet.

"See," she said. "Better, huh?"

"Yes," I said. "Sure."

Silence overtook us.

In general, I am a connoisseur of silence: I seek it out and enjoy it, and in social settings I use it to my advantage. In this instance, however, my mind raced uncomfortably, and I fetched about wildly for something to say. Something to fill the empty hole where words belonged. Something to plug the leak in our broken conversation.

I sprinted through empty fields in my mind and rushed over giant hills, grasping at long and wispy blades of grass, trying to grab hold of something—*anything*—I could say to this revelation in perfection, this goddess in the realm of everyday life, this rare and radiant lovely maiden whom the angels name Lenore.

Nameless here for evermore.

Lenore's soft voice shattered the silence. "My parents died on my seventeenth birthday."

Somewhere, a clock ticked. Somewhere, time disappeared.

* * *

The day was June 16, 2002. Sunlight pierced the clouds and warmed the earth, and the river crawled lazily through the outskirts of the city: London in the summer—like a fantastic poem awaiting its writer.

To celebrate her birthday Lenore had rented a punt and packed a picnic and called on her new friend from the States.

Lenore had met this young man five days prior, and they had taken a liking to each other in immediate and spectacular fashion.

"Not merely a romantic interest, either," she told me. "It was ... an interest that was different. Honestly, an interest that went beyond that. A connection—two like souls coming together and coexisting in harmonic perfection."

I'm not lying—those are the words Lenore used.

"I had asked him to come to the river that day along with a friend of mine—Jodie—and her boyfriend Mel. You see, he was there with his University, traversing Europe—something for credits for school—but he sneaked away from his professor, and he met us in the morning. It was damp and cool. I remember that. I remember that he hugged me when he arrived. My body felt so warm."

They had been on the river for a couple hours when they stopped and climbed ashore. The punt bumped against the land, and the four friends dug with leisure into the packed basket of food—sandwiches and a 'borrowed' bottle of wine—and a breeze danced across them, and the sweeping willow trees shaded them from the sun.

The sun was bright, and the day was bright, and everything was bright to Lenore.

"I would never live in America," she told the other three, and she took a bite of her sandwich.

"Oh, come now," her friend from the States said, "it isn't all that bad."

They smiled at each other.

His face radiated passion, and his eyes devoured Lenore and left her nearly swooning.

"Not so bad?" she said.

"It isn't. What do you think is so terrible about it?"

"America? It is a completely classless country. No one knows anyone. No one respects each other. No one cares about anything beyond their own preoccupations."

"Have you ever been to America?"

"Yes, as a matter of fact. I have."

"When?"

"Well. When I was eight. My father flew to New York for business, and I went with him."

"New York?" he said.

"Yes."

"No wonder you hate the States. New York is, like . . . the toilet bowl of the whole entire country."

"Where are you from?" Mel asked. He leaned forward. He held the bottle of wine by the neck. "You're probably from California, huh, mate?"

"No," Lenore said. "California boys are *way* hotter than him."

"Aw, Lenore," the boy from the States said, "that's a bit below the belt."

Lenore laughed.

The boy from the States laughed.

"I think you're positively *gorgeous*," Jodie said to the boy, and Mel spun and looked startled. "What?" she said to him. "You know I love you, baby. But he *is* gorgeous."

"As gorgeous as me?"

"Um . . ."

"I'm not from California," the boy from the States jumped in, saving Mel from embarrassment. "I'm from Colorado. And I go to school in Oklahoma."

"Never heard of them two, mate."

"You've never heard of *Colorado*?" Jodie asked.

"Isn't that what I just said?"

"How have you never heard of *Colorado*?"

"Bloody hell, I dunno. You'd never heard of the sixty-nine."

"Oh, that's completely different!"

"How so, huh? Explain it to me, babe."

"Oh, oh, I don't know, let me think—um . . . only that *Colorado* is like the equivalent of the *Alps*."

The American started to say something, but Lenore cut him off: "I'd like a cup of ice cream. How about a cup of ice cream, yes?"

They all looked at her.

"That would be pleasant," she said.

She pushed off the grass and snatched the mostly-empty basket from the blanket, then she walked to the water and dumped what was left of the food.

"Hey!" Mel called. "I was gonna eat that!"

"You don't need any more food," Jodie told him.

"Aw, c'mon, huh, whaddaya mean by that?"

"Nothing," she said. "Pick up that blanket."

They climbed in the punt and floated up the river.

Later that afternoon, after returning the punt (keeping quiet about the newborn crack in the pole, which the American had created when pushing off too hard from the bank of the river), the four young friends drifted through the narrow streets of the city on the clouds of their youth, fascinated by the magnificence of their surroundings and the careless beauty of the day.

Lenore studied the people who passed them. She looked at their smiles and their scowls, at their loveliness and their ugliness. She thought about how odd it was that all of these people had one thing in common: They each were alive, absolutely alive. They each breathed and moved and had thoughts and feelings and souls. Every person who passed them, no matter how different, was exactly the same.

Alive!

And what a gift it was.

The four of them ate ice cream with their feet in the Thames, and Lenore reached over and took hold of the American's hand. His palm sweated against hers. Neither of them seemed to mind.

They looked at each other, and he smiled. Rich brown hair falling in his eyes. The sun casting a shadow across his face—

Lenore leaned forward and kissed him. He kissed back. It lasted less than a second.

"Whoa, whoa!" Mel yelled. "Come off it, now, this isn't a private garden for Chrissake! This is the bloody city."

Jodie slapped his shoulder. "Don't you have any *decency*?"

"Not much," he said. He turned toward her. Lips locked. Lenore watched and laughed.

In the evening they rested, spread out in Hyde Park, all of them relaxing and sometimes sitting and telling stories, then lying down again. The tilt of the earth spun special for them.

The day was perfect.

Life was perfect.

The sun began to fall, and the American walked her home.

"We held hands while we walked," Lenore told me. "We held hands, and our arms swung together. Our feet moved together. Like we were made for one another."

They reached the house—a lovely Tudor mansion with decorative spires and decorative turrets and a wrought iron fence—and Lenore's grandfather, sallow and ancient, was sitting on the porch.

The two of them stopped. Lenore's head tilted, into a position of silent query. She watched her grandfather in all his majestic stillness.

His face looked somber. His eyes looked sad.

He glanced up and noticed her, and several seconds passed, and his brain registered what he was seeing. Two crinkled hands reached toward his knees, and he pushed until he rose to his feet. His back was bent from age. His feet pointed outward.

Somewhere, in the bushes, a thrush sang. No other sounds existed.

"Grandpapa?"

"Lenore." His voice climbed up from lungs that had lived through many hard-fought decades, that had survived three years of fighting in the Second Great War, that had held audiences captive and won many heated arguments. Lenore's grandfather was a venerable gentleman of passion and knowledge—a national treasure to the crown of England—and Lenore had never seen him looking so broken. Looking so sad.

"Grandpapa?" She started forward. The American hung back. "Grandpapa, what's wrong?"

"Lenore," he said. "Lenore." A tear appeared and peaked and tumbled from his eye. It crawled over his skin as gravity pulled it downward, leaving a trail of quickly-evaporated moisture.

Lenore ran toward him. He caught her in his arms.

"Grandpapa," she said. "Grandpapa, what's wrong?"

She knew the answer—oh, she knew; what else could it be?—but she asked nonetheless, grasping the straws of infinite and ever-unfailing hope.

"I'm so sorry," he said—whispered—into Lenore's ear. He pushed back her hair. Pressed his lips, dry and scratchy and cracked, against her sensitive skin. "I'm so sorry, pumpkin." She burst open, tears racing out of her eyes. "I'm so, so sorry."

"Grandpapa!"

They both cried, with the fervent passion of monumental loss.

Grandpapa: His son.

Lenore: Her parents.

The plane had hit a mountain.

* * *

Lenore looked at her knee, which had slipped out from the folds of the blanket. Her knee was distant from our conversation, but it was near enough to make her feel absorbed and close and focused.

I looked at her knee as well. There wasn't much else to look at.

"The American," Lenore said. She continued to stare at her knee—at the soft crinkles, which faded into smooth, white fields of bodily perfection. She reached forward. One slender finger brushed away at an imagined blemish. "I'm so sorry for doing this."

I replied with silence.

I forgive you, I wanted to cry. *Shhh, it's all okay!*

I wanted to hug her. To shower her with kisses.

"The American," she said. "His name was Jez Tagsam."

* * *

Two days after the tragic accident that stole Lenore's parents, the American students left London for Paris.

Jez stayed behind.

"Are you sure of it?" she asked him.

"I'm positive."

"I don't want you to get in trouble."

"It's all taken care of."

"You'll miss so many wonderful experiences."

"I have all the wonderful experiences I'll ever need, right here with you."

"You're sure?" she said again.

He kissed her on the cheek.

They stayed at Lenore's house, and Grandpapa stayed there also.

Grandpapa enjoyed Jez, and the two of them stayed up deep into the nights, discussing money and wars and world politics.

They drank brandy and smoked cigars, and Jez left these meetings feeling mentally exhausted.

"Say goodnight to Lenore before you retire," Grandpapa would say, and then he would leave for bed.

Jez would mount the stairs and step over the fifth step—which made an awful, spine-chilling creak if you touched it—and he would pad down the dark hallway until he found Lenore's room. Each night, she was already asleep. Each night, he knocked on the door and slipped silently into the room. Every night—as his feet crossed the moonlit floor—Lenore awoke. She kept her eyes closed, waiting for his words.

"Darling," he would whisper. "Darling."

"His whisper was so *magical*," Lenore told me, six years later while we sat together in front of a fire in a mansion on Nantucket Island, with her husband and his family all sleeping one house over and convinced that she was dead. "His whisper was so soft and calm, like the water in a tropical lagoon."

"Darling," he would say, then he would lean down and kiss her eyes.

She would open her eyes and smile. "Good evening, dear." She would rise onto her elbows. "How was your time with Grandpapa?"

"Exhausting," he would say.

Lenore would laugh.

"Fun, though. Fun. I really enjoy talking with him."

"He really enjoys talking with *you*."

Jez would pull back the blankets, and the cool moonlight would tumble through the window and dance across her body where its curves and shadows and promises of ecstasy shone beneath her nightdress, like fantastic secrets just barely out of reach.

Some nights she put her feet in his lap, and he rubbed them and caressed them. Sometimes his hands slid further up her legs, wrapping around her ankles, massaging her calves.

Other times she sat cross-legged, and Jez did the same—facing her like a mirror that did no justice to her beauty. On these nights he rested his hands on her calves while she leaned back against the headboard.

They talked for hours. They laughed and looked into each other's eyes and felt as close to one another as two people can feel.

One night he lay down beside her. They cuddled until the sun arose and spilled its light through the bottom of the window.

"Tell me about your family," she said.

"No," he said. "No, my family is so boring."

"Well. Tell me about your home."

Jez grew up on a ranch, in the mountains of Colorado. His mother worked hard. His father worked hard. Life was hard and dirty and devoid of romance or social glamour. His parents used to tell him, "Someday, son, this will all be yours."

When a private university in Northeast Oklahoma offered Jez a scholarship, he never looked back.

"Were your parents disappointed?"

"No."

"But didn't they want to give you the ranch? Didn't they want you to take over the family business?"

"What *business*? It's no *business*. It's a goddamn ranch."

"Don't cuss," Lenore said. "Don't cuss like that, I don't like it at all."

"I'm sorry."

"It's okay," she said.

"Is it?"

"Yes."

He leaned forward and kissed her.

Two weeks later, Jez left London with his classmates, and Lenore saw him off at the house.

"You'll write?" she asked him.

"Of course I will."

"You'll call?"

"Lenore, of course I will."

"I'm going to miss you."

"I'm going to miss *you*."

"All right, kids," Grandpapa said. "Let's get a move on, don't want to be late."

Lenore and Jez hugged. He kissed her cheek. Kissed her nose. Kissed her lips.

"Let's go, son. You're going to miss your flight."

Lenore kissed him back.

They let go, and he drifted to the car.

Grandpapa kicked the car to life, and he reached over and slapped Jez on the chest. "You're a good kid," he said.

Jez rolled down the window and leaned out of the car.

"I love you!" Lenore called. She walked slowly up the drive, her hair and dress and loveliness drifting behind her.

"I love *you*," he called.

They pulled onto the street, and she watched them disappear around the corner.

* * *

"I'm going to make a big request of you today," Lenore said. She gazed contemplatively through the emptiness of the room. "So I thought you ought to know something about me."

The fire behind us was nearly dead, and the blanket warmed our legs.

The whole world seemed contained inside that room with us. My whole world seemed hinged on each of Lenore's words.

"I know that Chas has . . ." she said. "I know he hasn't been faithful."

"I—"

"I know, Richard. I don't know who she is; I don't know what she looks like; I don't know why."

Her name was Lily Wrentsom. Maxwell had shown me a picture of her, and she was tall and blonde and buxom, and she had a plain, pretty face and dark eyes. As for why—well, I didn't have a clue.

"But I know," Lenore told me. "It hurts, Richard, I'm not going to lie. But he *is* my husband . . . "

"Yes."

"He *is*," she said, and she sounded nearly as if she was trying to convince me.

"I know."

"I left my plane, see? After I checked on—just before it took off, in fact. I left my plane. I had forgotten my . . . well. I'd forgotten something, and I needed it. So I ran off the plane and called Grandpapa, and he turned around to get me. The plane crashed. You know that. And I . . . oh God, Richard. Oh my *God*."

A lonely tear dribbled down the side of her face.

I reached over and wiped it away.

Lenore smiled.

"Thank you, Richard." Another tear emerged. The muscles in my legs tightened. "Thank you. You're pretty great."

"You know, Lenore. You don't have to tell me all this. If you don't want to."

"I'm okay. I'm okay to tell it."

"Are you sure?"

"I'm positive."

"Okay. Okay. Well, take your time."

Somewhere, a clock ticked. Somewhere, time disappeared.

"We were on our way to the market when the news broke over the radio. The plane had gone down, over the Atlantic. They knew no statistics yet, but the outlook was bleak . . . "

Grandpapa switched off the radio, and he pulled over onto the shoulder of the road. He looked at Lenore, and he saw that she was crying. He placed his hand on her back. His hand felt so warm, so *alive*, and Lenore . . . she felt so close to death.

"I kept thinking that if I had . . . you know, if I had only remembered to grab the . . . to grab the thing I forgot, my life would be over. I would be dead, Richard. It's a wild thought to deal with, right? Why does a thing like that happen to me? To me, and . . . not to all the other passengers? All of them are dead now. And I'm still alive."

She and her grandfather sat on the side of the road with traffic whizzing by—with his warm hand on the space between her shoulder blades—and her thoughts were clear, then her thoughts were muddled, then her thoughts were clear again. She realized: Maybe there was a reason. For all of this.

"Maybe I was supposed to . . ."

The soft hiss of the remaining embers, and the hint of a breeze brushing by Banucci Manor. The patter of raindrops clinking against the window. Otherwise: silence.

Lenore and I stared into the nothingness around us. The scene—the picture—that she had been painting for me was abruptly discontinued, half the canvas left blank, with wild strokes of color combining to create a portrait that was almost— *almost*—coherent . . . but not quite there.

I said nothing.

She tried to speak again, but her voice cracked and formed no words.

I kissed her cheek, and she hugged me, and the sides of our legs pressed tightly together.

"I'm so sorry to get you involved in this," she said. "I'm so, so sorry."

"Shhh," I said. "Shhh, it's all okay."

Her tears ran away from her and spilled and soaked my shoulder.

We stayed that way for a while.

Sometime later—with no new words yet spoken—we sat with space between us, and Lenore began to whisper through clenched teeth and intermittent drops of sadness.

My ears strained to hear her.

"I came back so I could see how . . . see how Chas reacted. See how he *reacts*. I'm dead, you see? And I know that it's wrong to do this, Richard, but I want to know how it goes. How the story plays out. How everything is at the funeral. I want to see how long it takes Chas to . . . to go and look for solace from his mistress. No, it's not right, but I *need* it, Richard. I need to know that I did the right thing. I need the release, and I'll leave, and I'll start my new life."

Lenore flew onto the island four days after the crash, on a private jet that Grandpapa had arranged—strings pulled, loopholes found. A perfect cat's cradle. A chauffer was waiting for her when she landed, and when nighttime fell and the world tucked in he drove her across the island and dropped her off up the road from Banucci Manor.

"Chas told me what a good guy you are," she told me, "while I was still back home. Back before I . . . died. He talked to me on the phone and told me how you were staying here, at Sandy's house, and he said . . . he said you seem like a quality man. Trustworthy. All that stuff. Richard, I'm so sorry, but that's why I'm asking you to do this."

Lenore wanted me to keep my eyes open. Keep my ears open. Pay attention.

She wanted to know how Chas reacted to her death.

She wanted to know how the family reacted.

She wanted to know how the world . . .

I looked at Lenore, and I thought how beautiful she was. I thought how deep her unseen interior was. I thought how perfect, how intangibly, unfathomably, mysteriously perfect, and . . .

"Sure," I told her. "Sure, Lenore. I'll help you however I can."

Lenore went to bed in a guest room upstairs, and I fell asleep in the chair at the desk in the study.

The rain continued to fall outside.

I couldn't write at all.

CHAPTER 5

Sunday morning was a flickering parade of names and faces that I barely registered or remembered—visitors from the island and the mainland who came to pay their respects, and who stuck around for the subdued romance afforded by tragedy. Most of the faces knew who I was, and Mamma Montana made it a point to clarify my importance with any who weren't aware of my occupation or reputation. "This is Richard *Park*land—the *wri*ter," she told them in her sincerest imitation of knowledge-able intimacy. "He was a finalist for the National *Book* Award."

They shook my hand, and I looked in their eyes and smiled and said hello.

All day long people filtered through the house, lending to the mammoth structure of stone and wood and glass a breath and a palpable heartbeat.

I met the Governor of Massachusetts (who had read my book) and the Mayor of Boston (who had not read my book, but knew who I was). I met the Mayor of Providence (who had read my book and claimed to be a big fan) and the President of Harvard (who, I was surprised to learn, had never even heard of me). With all of these names I made pointlessly whispered conversation.

I met Clara Ashley, the lovely actress from New Haven. I met Amory Cohn, the famous philanthropist and investment banker from Pennsylvania.

Most of these people had never met Lenore. Most of them knew Mr. Montana—knew Chas by reputation—and they fraternized and glowed, and they told their stories and conjured expressions of grief and loss.

These people made me sick, and I hid from them as best I could.

Maxwell hid also. He stayed in his room and smoked and drank. He passed the day in oblivion.

Finally, after a number of socially painful hours, I slipped through the throng of bodies—these people amongst whom I was nothing more than another uttered name—and I scaled the stairs and found his room and knocked on his door and entered.

"What's going *oooon*, brother?"

Maxwell was stoned.

"Not much," I told him. "Where have you been all day?"

"Just, uh. Hanging ou—just hanging out, man."

"Just hanging out?"

"Isn't that what I just said?"

"It is," I said.

"Nice."

Silence.

"What are you thinking about?" I asked.

For several moments Maxwell said nothing. He looked through the French doors, past the terrace and out toward the endless landscape of water and sky, and beauty and life, and liveliness, and fresh beginnings and bottomless possibilities, and—

"That's probably one of the emptiest questions in history," he said. Several more moments passed. "I was thinking about Lenore." He kept staring forward, but his attention shifted so it focused on me. "It all seems so official now, brother, with everyone here. I can't believe she's dead."

Words pushed against my chest. They tried to pry me open. They tried to escape into the cool, soft air.

I wanted to tell Maxwell that Lenore was alive, and that she was as gorgeous as anything in the world. I wanted to tell him that her voice was exactly the way he had described it—full of indescribable beauty. I wanted to say, Yes, Maxwell, yes, you were right—there is something *about* Lenore, something that can't quite be explained, something that makes you look in her eyes and feel enraptured as if nothing exists but her, and you could soar to the top of a mountain just so long as she never stopped looking at you. I wanted to tell him that Lenore was perfect, but I stopped. I suppressed my intrinsic inability to keep a secret, and I responded in emotionless fashion.

"Yeah," I said. "I can't believe it either."

"If you'd only known her—you would understand better."

"I . . . I'm sure. Yeah."

My mind left the house and crossed the grass and entered Banucci Manor. My mind saw Lenore, sitting upstairs with tea and a book and a blanket over her legs and breath in her body.

I understood how Maxwell felt. I understood, and I didn't understand at all.

He spun away from the doors and the terrace and looked at me like he was angry. "How shitty is this circus downstairs? None of these people care. None of these people even *knew* her."

"No."

"I don't mean *you*, brother. You—I mean . . . you didn't know her either, but. I didn't mean *you*. Shit. I just meant . . . "

He trailed off, and his words disappeared into the emptiness of the moment.

"Meant what?"

"Huh?"

"Nothing," I said. "Never mind."

We sat together on opposite sides of the room wallowing in the separate pools of our intertwined secrets.

"The *mayor*," he said—halfway to me, halfway to himself. "The *governor*. Neither of them knew Lenore. You know?"

"I know."

"And they act like they're all . . . here to just support us or, you know, whatever. Whatever, I only wish they'd all leave."

Honestly, Maxwell only wished that Lenore was still alive.

"Honestly," Maxwell said, "I only wish . . . "

Nothing.

* * *

The sand felt hard and dense and unforgiving beneath me. My toes were cold. I should have worn shoes.

Cecilia walked beside me. The wind had taken over her hair, and she smiled in that painful way in which a person will smile when they just want to make you happy.

"Are you okay?" she said. The words were mostly carried off on the wind, but she'd said them loud enough that I couldn't just ignore them.

"I'm fine."

"You're grimacing."

"Cecilia, I'm fine."

"Sorry. You were just real quiet and all. Then you were grimacing. I figured something was wrong. If you don't want to talk about it, it's no big deal."

"No, I'm—I was just thinking about something. That's all."

"Yeah?"

I didn't answer.

"Yeah," she said again. "You seemed a bit preoccupied. What's on your mind, huh?"

"Nothing."

"Well, obviously *some*thing is on your mind. You just said that you were thinking about something. Like I said, you don't have to talk about it if you don't want to. It's no big deal. Really, it's just—"

"I don't want to talk about it."

"Okay, fine. Geez, that's all you had to say."

The water crashed into the sand and ran toward us and slid away, and started over again. Crashed into the sand and ran toward us and slid away. Crashed into the sand and ran toward us—

"Does it have to do with my brother?"

"Which brother?"

"I don't know. Chas?"

"No."

"Does it have to do with Max?"

"No."

"Then . . . why did you ask 'which brother'?" she said.

I said nothing.

"It's just, if it didn't have to do with *ei*ther brother, you could've just said 'no.' Ya know?"

We walked in silence.

I found a rock and sat, and Cecilia sat beside me.

Away from clocks, away from schedules, away from everyday life, time died without ever actually existing.

"I'm sorry," she said. "I'm being nagging, I know. I get that way sometimes—Max used to always tell me that, and I'd always get angry with him, but he's absolutely right. I do. I don't know why, but I do, and I'm doing it right now. And I'm sorry."

"It's okay." I wasn't really listening to her. Maybe I thought about the grandiose ocean. Maybe I thought about the gathering inside The Palace that felt more like a political see-and-be-seen occasion than a mournful event. Maybe I thought about Lenore.

"It's just that you've seemed so *dis*tant," Cecilia was saying, "and I don't get to see you all too often, really, and now that I do, I—I'm . . . I want to spend some *time* with you, and get to talk to you and share with you and listen to your voice. And I hate to see you like this."

"Mmm." I wasted about three seconds trying to manufacture a response.

The waves kept crashing.

Time continued to die.

"I think I get this way when I'm cranky. I know it seems childish or corny or something like that. But, Richard, I'm just so *sad*. Over Lenore's death. And I really just am waiting for this whole thing to pass, for me to move on and for life to feel normal again. And I know it will, someday—someday soon, even—but right now it *feels* like nothing will ever be the same. Will ever be *nor*mal. Again. You would understand if you'd met her. I guess it's tough, though, for you to really grasp how we feel."

"Let's go back to the house," I said.

"Yeah? Do your feet hurt?"

I looked at them. "Some."

"I wish I could carry you," she said. I stood. Started walking. "Richard? *Ri*chard?"

I heard her stand up behind me.

The Palace was still full of moving bodies and serious voices when I returned. Entities who had shaken my hand earlier shook my hand again. Those who assumed I'd been close to Lenore offered their condolences. I saw Jez shaking hands and shaking his head and making whispered comments as well.

I pictured Jez, six years earlier—younger, with his hair a bit longer and his face maybe more full and of course just as handsome. I saw him in London, pulling the sheets back on Lenore's bed and the moonlight washing over them both and him sitting across from her holding her eyes and talking throughout the night. Their shared pasts. His secret. The mystery enshrouding him.

Jez noticed me across the room. He smiled at me. I smiled back.

How well had Jez known Lenore? I had asked him that, and he never answered.

There is nothing quite like a secret to make a man an island.

I felt for Jez, right then. I hoped he was doing all right.

The day dragged on.

Outside the walls of The Palace, across the grass, in the upstairs sitting room of Banucci Manor, Lenore sat alone reading—she waited for the gathering to dissolve, and for me to return home, and for me to report to her all the things I had seen.

In the evening the sun set and the world turned dark and the VIPs and distant acquaintances and shameless rubberneckers finally took their leave, the cars sliding like a hundred small fortunes up the driveway and off the grass and out onto the road, and I drifted through the spaciousness of the downstairs rooms, and Chas grabbed my arm and dragged me upstairs.

He plopped down on the couch.

I eased into a chair.

He started crying, and I said nothing, because I didn't know what to say.

"Why, Richard?"

"What's that?"

"You're the expert on life and all, right? Why do these things happen?"

"I . . ."

"I can't believe she's really dead. Richard, my God. If I could only have another chance, I promise. I'd make everything right. I swear I would! She was so perfect, so *amazing*. And I took her for granted and treated her poorly and . . . basically dumped all over her. Look where it got me. I'm a broken-down shell, and my wife is dead, and my life is in shambles."

"Shambles?"

"Yes, Richard. It really is."

"What about Lily?"

But Chas must have been drunk. Very drunk. He missed the rancor and sardonicism that I embedded inside of this question. Instead he took it as a perfectly normal query.

"Oh, Lily. What do I want with *Lily*? She's nothing, my friend. A fling. A...a toy, really. Don't tell her I said that."

"I won't."

"Yeah," he said. "Lily."

"Chas?"

He looked up.

"How can you say that, huh?"

"Say what?"

"About Lily."

"I..."

"It's just, I don't see how you can say, 'What do I want with *Lily*?' when you...you cheated on your wife with her. I mean..."

"You're absolutely right, Richard. Richard, old boy. It was a goddamn mistake. A huge goddamn mistake. Why did I ever go for Lily in the first place, right? I mean, isn't that what you're *saying*? And I don't have an answer, Richard, that's the goddamn crazy thing, I don't have an answer, because Lenore was everything a man could ever want in a woman, and I took her for granted and cheated on her and stomped her into the dirt, and now she's dead. And I'll never find another woman to replace her."

* * *

"He talked about finding a woman to replace you," I told Lenore that evening, after she asked about her husband.

"No—he didn't."

"He did."

"What did he say?"

"I don't know. Who knows? The typical stuff, I guess."

We were in the upstairs sitting room. We'd been sitting on the couch. She stood and walked forward so the back of her head faced me.

"You're kidding—right? Richard, please. Tell me you're kidding."

"I'm . . ." I said. "I wish I could. I can't, though. I'm not kidding."

"I don't believe this."

She paced toward the wall. Turned around. Paced toward me and turned away and paced toward the wall again.

"Can't you remember *anything* of what he said?"

"I just remember those words, honestly—'. . . find another woman to replace her.' Those were his exact words. I'm at least certain of that."

Lenore kept pacing. Back and forth, back and forth. She looked lovely, framed inside the wide window with the dark night and the distant sounds of the ocean stretching out beyond her.

"That's all you remember, Richard?" She looked at me while she paced. "That's all you remember? Nothing more?"

"I'm sorry. This is all just such a whirlwind for me."

"I know. I feel awful for even dragging you into this."

"Don't feel awful, Lenore. It isn't your fault."

"No. No, it is."

"How is this your fault?" I said.

Lenore stopped pacing. She gazed at the window. Maybe she could see the ocean. Maybe she gazed at her reflection. "How can you even ask that, Richard?"

"I like when you say my name. It sounds lovely with your accent."

"Richard."

"Yes?"

"If I would have just called the family and told them I was alive—told them I was okay—you would never have been dragged into all this. My goodness, Richard, if I'd even just stayed home—never come back here at all—none of this would have happened. Everything would go back to normal, and none of this would have happened."

I stood also. I didn't know what to do with my hands, so I shoved them into my pockets. "Lenore. Lenore, look at me. If Chas hadn't treated you the way he did, you would never have thought to do this in the first place. It isn't your fault, it can't be. If you had a husband who treated you the way you *deserve* to be treated . . . if you . . . you would have wanted to come home to him, if your husband treated you right."

"How *do* I deserve to be treated?" she said.

"You . . ." I stopped. I looked at the ceiling in the corner of the room. "You deserve to be treated like a princess, Lenore. You deserve to be treated like the most amazing woman alive."

"Yes. But . . . what does that even mean, Richard?"

I slid my hands from my pockets. My feet carried me across the hardwood floor. When I reached Lenore, I waited for her to look up. But she didn't. My lips touched her forehead.

"Lenore."

"Yes?"

"You are an incredible woman."

"Yes . . ."

"You're gorgeous. You're intelligent. You're sweet and—and strong—and lovely to be around. You're a fantastic woman, Lenore. Any man who couldn't see that—who couldn't *treat* you as such—any man who . . . who would *cheat* on you. Lenore.

Who would betray your trust. Any man like that was . . . wasn't worth the breath in his body. He . . . "

"How poetic," she said. She laughed. Her laugh was reassuring.

"Sorry."

"No. No, I like it. Keep going."

"Look at me, Lenore."

"I can't."

"Why?"

Lenore looked at me. Our gazes collided.

"Because," she said, "when I look in your eyes I feel alive. I haven't felt that in so long, Richard." She leaned toward me a fraction. My heart beat faster. "I feel alive, and it scares me."

Somewhere, time stood still.

Another fraction of empty space—shoved away. Inching, inching toward each other in tandem movements of microscopic size and cosmic importance. She wore a perfume that smelled faintly of peach. I wondered, faintly, if Chas had bought it for her.

I felt like Lenore could read my thoughts.

I thought of nothing but her.

Fields of happiness stretched on and on before me—running and dancing and leaping—all the way into a slow-setting sun that shined rays of pure contentedness all over and throughout the landscape of my life.

I felt the tension between us—the air compressing and disappearing as my lips drifted toward hers.

Eye contact.

Bracing.

Impact in 10

9

8

7

Impact in 6
In 5
In 4
3
2
Halt.
Noise downstairs.
Someone yelling, calling my name.

* * *

"What should I do?"

The air between us shuddered. We held our position with lips almost touching. Eyes holding each other closer than darkness holds the night.

Beneath us: "Richard!"

Moving closer: "Richard!"

Heading toward the stairs: "Richard!"

"Hide," I said.

She held still, and I waited.

She touched my chest. Her face moved away.

"Hide where?" she said.

"Richard!"

"Hide...hide...stay in here." Her hands: still on my chest. Our eyes: still locked together. (Downstairs: "Richard? Richard!") "Stay in here, I'll lead him somewhere else."

I started to turn.

"No!" Lenore said. She grabbed my arm.

Approaching: "Richard!"

"He's on the stairs," she said. "He'll want to come in here," she said. "I *know* him," she said. "This is where he'll want to come."

"You're sure?"

Closer: "Richard! Where are you, man?"

"I'm going into the hallway."

"He'll see you!"

"Riiichaaard."

"He won't, I promise."

"Richard? Come on, brother. Where the hell are you?"

The door clicked shut behind her.

"Richard?"

I hopped onto the couch and closed my eyes and pretended to fall asleep.

Creeeak, the door opened. Maxwell's feet sloshed across the floor.

"Richard? *Richard*? Riiiicha—oh! *There* you are."

I peeled my eyes open.

"Whoa, you been sleeping, brother? I been looking all over for you."

"Ohhh, yeah," I said. I stretched and yawned. "I *have* been sleeping. Napping. What time is it?"

"I need to talk to you, man." Maxwell sank into the couch. I dragged my feet out from underneath his legs. "Oh," he said. He looked at my feet. "Sorry."

"No problem."

I heard noise in the hallway. I saw Lenore's face. The door clicked shut again.

"You were saying?"

Maxwell said nothing. He stared straight ahead, at the window—and beyond the window, the infinite length of ocean.

The vase from the coffee table flew across the room and hit the wall and shattered and tinkled to the floor.

He jerked his head away. Tears fell off his face. I continued to sit still.

I said nothing.

Maxwell said nothing.

Finally, I said: "Maxwell?" There was nothing else to say.

He stared at his reflection in the window and grimaced. His self-hatred flooded the empty space where conversation should have existed.

"Maxwell."

"———— off."

"Hey. Look at me," I said. He didn't. "Maxwell, look at me. I'm on your side, man." I tried to catch his eyes in the mirror of the window.

"No one is on my side."

"That's not true—"

"It is true, Richard. Don't you understand? Don't you get what this is like? No one knows how I feel right now. No one *gets* it, brother."

Maxwell reeked of alcohol and marijuana. The things he said came from deep inside himself—words he would have suppressed were he not so mood-and-mind altered.

"Come on," I said. "Stop that, Maxwell—stop it right now. Get a hold of yourself."

"———— off," he said again, whispered. "———— everyone, Richard. Nothing matters anymore."

Outside the door, a floorboard creaked.

"Why would you say that, Maxw—"

"Goddammit, Rich. Stop it, brother—just *shut up.*"

"Maxwell, I——" I reached out and touched him.

"Stop it! Don't do this to me, Richard. Everything is falling apart. Don't you get it? I'm in the goddamn middle of this goddamn storm. And *everything is falling apart.*" He stood. He teetered. "Augh, I'm sick of it, Richard! I'm so damn *sick* of it."

"Sit down," I told him.

Maxwell didn't listen.

"I hate it. I *hate* it."

He stumbled forward. He grabbed one end of the coffee table. He heaved, and he flipped the coffee table over.

The coffee table skidded and rattled and came to rest.

He lunged forward and grabbed the legs and—*Aoough*, with effort—drove the coffee table across the room.

It met the wall, and Maxwell's body kept moving. He tumbled off his feet and landed in a heap inside of the upturned table.

He struggled to his feet and hit the wall with his open palm.

He lost his balance, and he tumbled into the coffee table again.

I sat on the couch, not moving. Hands folded over my stomach.

"Maxwell."

"Go to hell."

"Maxwell."

He stared down at his legs. "I'm so sorry, brother. God, I'm so damn sorry. It's all falling apart, man. Everything in my life."

Somewhere, a clock ticked. Somewhere, time disappeared.

Somewhere, in the hallway, a floorboard creaked.

"She's dead, brother. Don't you understand that? She's dead, Richy. I'll never see her again."

"Shhh," I said. "Shhh. It's all okay."

"It isn't okay." He held his face in his hands. "It's not, really. Don't you understand it?" His back rose and fell. I think he cried. I think his eyes poured tears, and he caught them with his fingers.

"Shhh."

"Oh, Richard. I planned it for so long. For so damn *long*. Before my brother ever proposed to her, I was going to tell her how I felt. Before my brother married her. Before their one-year anniversary . . . after I found out that Chas was cheating on her. Before she left for London, just a couple weeks ago. All those times."

"How . . . " I started. "How *do* you feel?"

The room felt like a vacuum.

Maxwell either said, "Huh?" or he made a noise that sounded similar.

Either way, I repeated my question.

"How do I feel about what?" he said.

"You just said that all those times you planned to tell her how you felt, Maxwell. So . . . ?"

He looked up, and our eyes clashed, and everything in our worlds seemed to finally come together. "I love her," he said. "I never stopped loving her," he said. "All the way until she died."

"She isn't dead," I said.

Outside the room, a floorboard creaked.

* * *

Cecilia came over that night. I caught her at the door, and I grabbed her arm, and I moved her toward the beach.

"It's cold outside."

"Don't worry about it," I said.

Cecilia and I walked and didn't talk.

I found a spot to sit.

We sat beside each other and watched the waves where they crashed and faded.

"You've been weird lately, Richard."

I kept watching the waves. I didn't feel like talking.

"Richard?"

The ocean looked black. The ocean looked like it held every answer to all the questions that were killing us.

"Richard, how come you've been so weird lately?"

"It's just . . . " I said. I kept my eyes on the water. "It's just because of my writing."

After I began working on my first novel I found that this excuse comes in handy with fortunate frequency. Anything goes wrong?—blame it on troubles with your writing. Treat someone poorly?—blame it on your preoccupations with writing. Forget an important event?—once again: writing.

Best of all (worst of all?), Because Of My Writing covers every bad attitude and lapse in general courtesy—one of the perks of being a writer.

"What's going wrong with your writing?" Cecilia said. She picked at the sand between us.

"Nothing," I said. "Nothing is *wrong*, necessarily. Things have just been tough lately [True], and . . . it's all I can really think about right now [False]."

"You don't want to tell me what's been tough with it?"

"No."

"Why not?"

"Because, Cecilia. You wouldn't be able to help me. And besides, I—"

"Why would you say that, Richard? How is that supposed to make me feel?"

"Wait, how—how is *what* supposed to make you feel?"

"Oh," she said, mocking my voice, "*you* wouldn't be able to help me."

"Whoa, Cecilia . . . what?"

"*You*'re just an idiot,"—still mocking my voice—"*you* can't help me at all."

"That's not even——" I said. I stopped. I stood. I walked back toward Sandy's house.

"That's not even what?"

I didn't answer.

Cecilia didn't follow me. She stayed on the beach with the water hitting the sand and running toward her feet and falling back upon itself before starting over again.

* * *

Moonlight trickled through a sliver of space between the closed curtains. I sat on the edge of the bed, and I stared into the speaking shadow whose name was Lenore.

"It took everything inside of me to not barge into that room and give Max a hug, and tell him that I'm alive. I feel so *awful*, Richard."

"It's all just a part of it."

"What is?"

"All of this. The things you're dealing with right now. It's all just a part of this."

"It's so tough."

"Even still," I said. "I contend that you're doing the right thing."

"Richard."

"Yes?"

"That's not enough anymore."

"What's not enough?"

"The 'right thing.' Besides. It doesn't even feel like I *am* doing the right thing."

"We can't base our judgments off of feelings," I said.

"That's easy for you to say," she said.

I bit my tongue.

She had no idea...

"I never had any idea before how much Max cares for me. He said such wonderful things."

I sat perched there on the edge of the bed. I kept watching her silhouette and waiting for her words.

"I only planned to listen outside the door for a minute. But he said such *wonderful* things. And he showed such a fiery passion when he spoke of me. I couldn't help but stick around."

"Yeah. I don't think he's doing so well," I said.

"I only wish I could do something to help him."

"He broke the vase from the coffee table."

"I heard it hit the wall."

"It was a nice vase."

"Believe me," Lenore said, "the Banuccis won't even notice."

Earlier in the evening, when I said to Maxwell that Lenore was not dead, he nodded and agreed—still slumped against the wall, inside the palm of the upturned coffee table.

"I know," Maxwell said. "We have our memories. The world has the mark she left. She has her spirit. All those things live on, I know. But it's . . . it's easy to say those things in theory, brother. It's easy to say that to someone who's experienced loss. But it sure doesn't temper the pain."

"No," I said. I whispered. "Maxwell. Lenore is still alive." But I said it too quietly for Maxwell to hear.

"What's that?" he said. "Oh, never mind. It doesn't matter anyway."

The muscles in one of my thighs quivered.

Maxwell watched the floor.

I watched it too.

"What am I supposed to do, Richard? I need your help. Look, I feel shitty for treating you so bad. I didn't mean to yell at you and all. I really didn't, you—you're the only person I really trust right now. You're the only person I can turn to. And I'm screwing everything up so royally. I just want all of this to pass. To end." The room breathed along with us. I waited for him to continue, and he waited for the exact same thing. "I just want to close the book on all of this, and forget all of this, and move on with my life."

After Lenore and I quit talking about Maxwell, I moved closer to her, and I held her feet and massaged them gently, and the sliver of moonlight played across her body—shifting from her stomach to her chest, and back to her stomach again.

For a time, we sat without speaking. The silence rained down on us like a spring shower so light and so lovely that you and your lover leave the protection of the roof above you and run through the rain holding hands and laughing and feeling full of bliss. Nothing satisfied me more than that silence.

When Lenore spoke, nothing satisfied me more than her words.

I have thought back to that night many times since I left Nantucket; that night stands out to me like a highlight of happiness buried inside all the horrible things that happened in the end.

What did we talk about?

What did she say?

I have no idea.

In that way, Lenore was always like a dream—something you awake from and wish desperately that you could return to, but by the time you begin brushing your teeth or step into the shower you no longer have any idea what the dream was about at all. The only thing you know is: You wish that you could go back.

It annoyed me, early on, when I heard so often: If only you had met Lenore. Yes, I thought, but what exactly was so amazing about her? None of you have told me.

But everything they told me was true.

Lenore's voice. Her voice cast a spell over you. You heard her voice and felt like your feet were lifted off the ground.

Lenore's eyes. They were more than just the color of pool-blue. They were like pools themselves. They pulled you in—not like those haunting eyes that pierce you and seem to bore into the places you wish to hide, but rather, Lenore's eyes enveloped you. They wrapped around you and made you feel like she knew you better than you knew your own self, and all the while you felt safe. Comfortable. At ease.

Lenore's face. She looked like a picture escaped from the cover of a magazine—an already-beautiful celebrity who has had every blemish airbrushed and each imperfection perfected. Lenore was no man's "Type"—she was an everywoman, who appealed to every man. Like an angel. Like a muse. I imagine it would be impossible for any man to look at Lenore and not fall in love, and not think she was the most beautiful woman they had ever seen in their life.

Lenore's personality. Personality itself is too small and too drab a word to describe Lenore's persona. Personality is what other people—mortals—employ in order to portray who they are. Lenore . . . she was just simply She. She was simply magic.

You would understand if you'd met her.

Lenore was everything. She was anything you wanted her to be.

Sometimes I think back and wonder whether Lenore existed at all. Perhaps we invented her ourselves. Perhaps she was only an idea.

Lenore told me to move closer to her that night, and I scooted up the bed. She put her legs over mine. She held my eyes. She told me stories. She listened when I spoke.

She fell asleep in the early hours of the morning, and I pulled the sheets out from under her and covered her and stood in the doorway before I left.

The great Lenore slept soundly.

I went to my room and thought of Lenore and slept soundly also.

I awoke on Tuesday morning to the sound of heavy pounding on the front door of Banucci Manor.

CHAPTER 6

"Jez! How are you?"

"We need to talk."

"Come in."

He had already pushed past me and entered the foyer.

"Sorry for waking you," he said.

"Oh, you're—"

"I hate to barge in like this, I couldn't hold this in any longer, though, it's just chewing away at me."

I stood watching him like a house left barely standing by a sudden storm.

He leaned around the corner. Searched about. Disappeared toward the kitchen.

I followed. I rounded the entrance to the kitchen and ran into him on his way back out.

"Sorry, sorry," he said. He held my shoulders and scooted by me and avoided my eyes.

"Jez. Are you oka—"

"I'm really sorry, Richard. So much going on right now. So much going on."

"Jez."

"I'm not usually like this. Really, I'm not. I couldn't stand it any longer, though."

I followed him toward the living room. He bumped into me again.

"Oops, sorry about that. Forgive me, Richard."

"Yeah, Jez. No problem. Wha—"

"Just so much going on. I'm trying to process it all and deal with it all and it's beginning to be too much. I don't know how much longer I can hold up under all of this pressure. Sit down, sit down, Richard. You're really making me nervous."

"Look—"

"Look at me, my hands are shaking. Sit, *sit*." He kept talking as I eased into the salmon-colored chair.

Outside of the window the morning sun shone brightly—skipping across the water and dancing over the sand and running up the grass until it tumbled through the window.

I barely noticed.

I watched Jez, and I wondered where he was going.

" . . . just all over the place, if you know what I'm saying. So frenetic, just bouncing every which-way. I wish I could put a leash on it, really—on my thoughts, at least—but you can't do that, and I'm feeling so overwhelmed with it and it seems like this is my only recourse, and I hate to do this, Richard, because I promised I wouldn't but what else can I do at this point when it seems like no other options exist to me and I'm falling so deeply under all this shit that's going on, it just makes me want to scream is what it makes me want to do, and if I could only get over this hump and somehow *see* the finish line I think I'd be okay, but it all seems so distant right now I don't think I'll ever get there and it doesn't seem like there's any end in sight to all this madness and I'm afraid that if this doesn't end soon I'll—"

"Jez! *Breathe*."

"—running around until I finally *do* find the answers or *do* find the end and you can't force things like this—you really can't—if there's one thing I've learned it's that, but it's so incredibly hard to keep on with this when it seems like a better option would be—"

"Jez!"

"Yes?"

I tried to hold him steady with my eyes.

"Stop," I said. "Breathe."

"Rich—"

"It's all okay. I don't know what you're saying, but geez, man, it's all okay."

His shoulders hung lower. He breathed in, deeply. He closed his eyes. He said: "Okay."

"Just . . . just calm down," I said.

"Okay."

"All you need is—"

"Hello, Jez." My eyes jerked toward the door.

Lenore.

In shadow. Her voice rising from the shadow, like a balloon climbing toward heaven.

Her eyes shining.

Her dark hair cascading over her shoulders.

She took a step forward.

"Hello," Jez said, choking on the word.

"Aren't you going to give me a hug?" she said. She took another step forward.

"Yes," Jez said. "Yes, I am."

"Well? Come on with it, then."

He walked toward Lenore, as if learning to walk on air.

They met.

They hugged.

Her hands came together at the back of his head with her fingers buried in his hair, and he held her tight, and I stared and said nothing.

* * *

Love spans miles. Love spans years. Love spans chasms hewn from the rocks of separation and intrusion and the dying embers of memories long-forgotten.

I stumbled through the grass, then I stumbled through the sand.

Clouds of frustration and anger and betrayal eddied off behind me, and the same clouds lay before me. The same clouds wrapped their cold, iron claws around me, scraping over my veins and shuddering through my nerves.

I shoved my gaze deep into the sand—the sand, a collection of sheared and shaved particles that used to be boulders, then used to be stones, then used to be rocks before they became pebbles and then became this. Thousands of years of constant bombardment, of waves crashing upon them until life rubbed off them and the pieces were shorn away.

These particles leaped from the earth and sifted into my shoes.

From the dust we were formed, to the dust we return.

And so much literary rambling boils down to this: Those weeks in Nantucket impacted my life in such a profound manner as to render word-based definitions difficult if not entirely impossible. But words are my life—so I try hard, and I do the best I can.

Words.

Sometimes so empty. And yet, so often, our only bridge to concreteness and meaning amongst the slosh that comprises our lives.

I finally reached the shore—on that cold and blustery morning that seems so far away from me right now, but which also seems near enough that I could touch it if I only cared to reach out with my fingers (which, incidentally, I *don't* care to do)—and I sat on a rock that would someday become a pebble and would someday become a million grains of sand, and I watched an osprey dive toward the ocean. What a pointless life it leads, I thought—a life comprised of nothing more than food and shelter and flying.

What a pointless life I lead, I thought.

A life comprised of nothing more than food and shelter and stories...and a desperate search for meaning inside the muck and mire of a muddy existence.

The waves crashed, over and over. Some would say incessantly. *I* would say incessantly. Never ending. Never resting. Over and over again. How tiresome! How boring!

How beautiful.

The infinite immutability of things much greater than ourselves.

I watched the water where it landed in the sand. I watched the water where it met the sky. I imagined London in the unseen distance—miles and weeks and imaginations away from the spot in which I sat.

Inside of Banucci Manor, Lenore and Jez talked.

I sat alone, and I waited.

* * *

"Darling, could you pass the butter, please."

Chas fingered his face and wiped away a tear, then he grabbed the plate of butter. He leaned over his sister and handed the plate to Mamma. He reached for his face again.

"Are you okay, Chas?"

"I'm fine."

"Are you sure? Do you need to go lie down?"

Chas didn't answer. He stabbed his fork into a pile of hash browns, and most of them fell from the fork and tumbled back onto the plate. He shoved the fork into his mouth and swallowed what was left there.

"Chas. Did you h—"

"He's fine, dear."

"Well, *Charles*," she said to her husband. Her voice was hushed and sharpened. "I'm only trying to help the boy, he's really broken apart."

"It sure doesn't help for you to coddle him like this." He kept eating. His face looked passive, like this was a normal conversation.

"I'm not *cod*dling him. I'm only trying to *help* him, to guide him through this."

"Guide him? Sweetheart,"—bite, swallow—"you're not doing any better than he is."

"Well, Mr. Stony-face, excuse me if I'm not as in*sen*sitive as *you* are. We can't all be so cold-*heart*ed."

"Cold-hearted?" He set his fork down. He wiped the corners of his mouth with his napkin. He tossed the napkin onto the table. "Cold-hearted, right. And what on earth are you then, my dear? A large pile of squash?"

"Well! I've had near about enough of this!"

"Have you?"

"I sure *have*," she said.

Chas pushed his chair back. He stood. He dragged his feet behind him, and he escaped from the room.

"Well there you go," Mr. Montana said. "Are you happy now?"

"Am I—am *I* happy? *You're* the one who ran him off!"

"Oh, please. That," he said, pointing, "is not my fault."

Cecilia ate in silence.

Maxwell ate in silence.

Mamma Montana shut her mouth and began to eat in silence.

No one spoke. We all just cut and stabbed and shoved and chewed, and we waited for time to pass.

"Has anyone seen Jez?" Mr. Montana said. "I haven't seen him for several hours."

"I haven't seen him either," Mamma agreed. "Does anyone know where he is?"

I focused on my plate. I cut and stabbed and shoved and chewed.

* * *

Before his senior year of college Jez took out a student loan for several thousand dollars. He did not need the money for school—his scholarship covered him there. Instead, he used the money to take a trip to London.

He flew there for fall break.

Grandpapa picked him up at the airport.

"Jez."

"Mr. Watson. How are you, sir?"

They shook hands.

"I'm doing well, Jez, I'm doing well. I'm glad you could make it out here—Lenore speaks of you constantly."

"Oh. I hope she doesn't bore you with me."

"Not at all."

"Well, sir, I'm excited to be here."

They drove to his house in the country, and Lenore met the car halfway between the front door and the ivy-covered fence. Jez climbed out, and she leaped into his arms.

"Oh, Jez! I'm so happy you're here."

They went to dinner that night in London, and after dinner they walked to the river and dipped their feet in the water, in the same spot where they had sat and dipped their feet in the water on that sunny day in the summer. Back in simpler times.

They talked about Jodie and Mel. They held hands and walked through the city and made up stories about the people who passed them. They kissed outside the gates of Buckingham Palace. They were quiet together. They enjoyed being quiet together.

At Hyde Park they laid in the grass beside The Serpentine with their arms entwined like serpents, and they counted the stars, and were happy.

They didn't return home until the night waned old and the life of the city petered out around them.

When they stepped inside the house, Grandpapa called to Jez from the sitting room.

"Yes, sir?"

"Why don't you come in here."

"Yes, sir."

"Come upstairs when the two of you are finished," Lenore said. She kissed Jez on the cheek, and she slipped upstairs.

"Lenore," he whispered. "Lenore." He put his hand on her leg and squeezed, just a little bit. "Wake up, Lenore." She opened her eyes. "You awake, precious? You wanted me to come up here when I finished talking with your grandfather. Here, go back to sleep."

She squinted at him. The room was mostly dark. "Are you two done talking?"

"We are."

"How was your chat?"

"Pleasant. Exhausting."

"As usual," she said.

"As usual."

"Here, lie down beside me."

"I don't want to keep you from sleep."

"Jez."

"Okay." He kicked his shoes off, then he climbed into bed.

Lenore curled her body into him, and he put his arm around her. Both of them fell asleep, and both of them were happy.

Their week disappeared in a flash of romance and splendor and late nights of cuddling and kissing and revelations of deepest thoughts and dreams and secrets.

And then, Jez left.

He returned to America, and his world seemed mundane. Bleak. Empty.

Lenore remained in England, and she passed the days reading and lounging in the sun, waiting for Jez to call.

She had already finished sixth form in the spring, and she had been accepted to University of Oxford. But now, she was taking a year off to let the pain of her parents' death sink in and filter out and become nothing more than memory.

After Jez left London and returned to the States, Lenore decided to apply to Harvard. She made this decision on a whim. She made this decision with no consideration for the future that this action might create.

In the spring, she received a letter of acceptance. She told her grandfather that she was going to leave England and travel to America.

"You're sure?" Grandpapa asked her.

"I am."

"Absolutely?"

"No," she said.

"Why not?"

"I don't think you can ever be absolutely sure."

"Of what?"

"Of anything."

"Ah. Such wisdom," Grandpapa said.

"You're okay with me going?"

"Sweetheart."

"Yes?"

"I approve of whatever you decide."

Lenore leaned up, and she kissed him on the cheek. "You're the best, Grandpapa."

"I know."

"The absolute best."

She called Jez and told him.

"That's so wonderful," he said.

"I know. You and I will be able to see each other all the time, now."

"Lenore . . ."

"Yes?"

"America is a big country."

"Oh. Yes."

"But hey, maybe I'll get a job up near Boston. And then we *would* see each other all the time."

"I hadn't thought of that."

"Hadn't thought of what?"

"What a large country America is. How far away Boston is from Colorado."

"Well. Believe me, I *won't* be going back to Colorado."

"What if you end up in California?"

"I won't."

"What if you do? That's so far from Boston, Jez—the only reason I'm *coming* to America is so I can be with you."

"Lenore, I won't end up in California. Listen, don't let me put a damper on your excitement—you're going to attend Harvard, dear. There aren't many things that could be more exciting."

"I know," she said. "Oh, I know. Jez. You'll look for a job in Boston?"

"If I can get one."

"You'll look?"

"Of course I will."

"I'm scared to move there if I don't know anyone."

"I'll look for a job in Boston."

"And you'll find one?"

"I'll do my best."

"Promise me that you'll find a job in Boston, Jez."

"I don't make promises."

"Oh yes. I forgot."

"But I'll do everything within my power to find a job in Boston."

"Can you at least promise *that*?"

"Yes, Lenore. I at least promise that."

Jez painted the city with his résumé.

One week later he heard back from Montana Inc., and they flew him to Boston for a formal interview.

One week after the interview, Montana Inc. offered him a position. They asked him if he preferred to work at the Providence branch or in Boston.

Boston, he told them. Definitely Boston.

One month after Jez moved to Boston, Lenore came to Harvard.

* * *

Jez and Lenore shared transition periods in much the same way that spouses share a bank account—everything went into a single location, and everything came out of the exact same place. His trials and joys and experiences became hers, and hers became his.

Two lives became one.

During that first year they took it upon themselves to discover the city together.

Thursday nights they reserved for restaurants. Friday nights for bars. Saturday nights for out-of-the-ordinary—whether it be theatre or opera or ballet or baseball. Sunday nights were set aside for relaxing, for clearing their minds and enjoying each other without distractions.

They didn't officially date each other throughout that first year, but neither did they need to. Time was open before them like a boulevard at night, and they drove with the top down, enjoying the air. They had decided to use that year to become intimate with each other as persons. To use that year as a construction site, on which they were building the foundation of a relationship that would tower above the most romantic relationships in history.

Jez discovered every detail—both public and private—about the great Lenore, and in exchange he opened to her every room within his Fortress of Self.

They loved each other.

They were happy.

They had discovered their permanent world.

Lenore adjusted magnificently to the Harvard life, entrenching herself amongst all the best people. She had a natural way with those of the same sex, coming across as pleasant and friendly and approachable, as completely grounded and down-to-earth.

As I sit in the dark—with whiskey on the table beside my open computer, and with the whole of central Paris spread out beneath my open window—it occurs to me that it is difficult to define why, exactly, women were so drawn to Lenore. It is generally understood that if one woman is physically stunning, most other women hate her. Perhaps this stems from competition. Perhaps this stems from insecurities. Perhaps this stems from the plain and simple truth that no one can quite understand and define the female brain. Somehow, however— and I certainly don't know *how* Lenore pulled it off, as I was not around to observe and document and hypothesize—women loved Lenore almost as much as men loved her.

Maybe women saw Lenore and despised her at first, because she was lovely to such an unfair degree. But they met her, and she was the opposite of any negative attribute they could possibly have ascribed her. She was everything they wanted her to be, and she was everything they wanted to be themselves. She was friendly and calm and smart and well-spoken. She was wise and knowing. She was strong. Women felt comfortable around her. They felt accepted and loved. They felt close to her, and this closeness lent credibility to their own unstable and insecure lives.

As for men...well, that's a bit easier to define. When she passed men on campus they looked at her and ogled. They smiled at her. They watched her walk until she walked too far away for them to watch her any longer. And while most men were too intimidated to approach Lenore, those who dug up the courage discovered that she was more incredible than her looks. She made them feel important and absolutely level, in spite of her overwhelming aura.

Of course...there *were* some (a lot, I'm sure) who muscled up and asked her on dates, and these men walked away from their moment of bravery feeling like a fool. Lenore, however—wonderful woman that she is—did all she could to temper the blow. "I'm sort of seeing someone right now. Sorry."

"Oh, no. No, *I'm* sorry—it's okay, I'm sorry—don't worry about it."

"Sorry," Lenore would say again.

"Sort of seeing someone?" Jez used to laugh. "What is *that* supposed to mean?"

Lenore would laugh too. "I don't know. I'm not really sure."

"How can you be 'sort of' seeing someone? Either you are seeing someone, or you aren't."

"That's not true, Jez. Look at us."

"What about us?"

"You and I aren't seeing each other. Right?"

"Of course not. Not at all." He would wink at her. "You and I are just friends."

"Right." Pause. "But we decided—*together*—to not date other people."

"Sure."

"We decided—*together*—to use this year as a means by which to ... to get to know one another. To prepare ourselves for the *oh*-so-perfect relationship we'll have together in the future. So— you get it? 'Sort of' seeing someone."

"I guess. Yeah, I get it."

"Good."

"*I'm* the person you're sort of seeing?"

Lenore would laugh.

"Okay," Jez would say. "Just trying to clear that up."

Lenore returned to England that next summer, and she and Jez continued to talk for hours each day. Deepening. Widening. Strengthening the canal through which their shared waters flowed.

When they talked to one another the two of them discussed the future they imagined themselves sharing—the home in which they would live, the kids they planned to create. The experiences they would enjoy and places they would explore.

Every so often Grandpapa grabbed the phone from Lenore, and he lectured Jez on politics and military tactics and current world events. He would hand the phone back to Lenore, always leaving Jez with something like this: "Keep driving forward, Jez, don't ever stop. You're a brilliant mind, and you'll always be able to accomplish and achieve anything you can dream. I'm telling you the truth, young man—you're a rare breed like that. Don't you ever stop running, and don't ever stop dreaming. Now talk to my granddaughter, okay? Make sure you treat her well."

"Sorry," Lenore would say.

"I don't mind."

"I know you don't."

"Really, I don't mind. I promise. I love your grandfather."

"I know you do," Lenore would say.

"I really do. You know why?"

"No. Why?"

"Because your grandfather is an important part of your life. Anything that's important to you is equally important to me."

"That's sweet."

"It's true." Their conversations were like that.

Their conversations were like lots of things, but mostly their conversations were like an escape from a world in which neither of them was whole, neither of them was complete, because neither of them was with the other.

At the end of July Jez took one week of vacation and flew to England, and Grandpapa picked him up at the airport and drove him to the house.

"Lenore!" Jez called. He stood in the entrance hall of Grandpapa's grand house, and he called again. "Lenore! Surprise..."

Lenore *gallumped* down the stairs. She *whooshed* into his arms.

"Oh, Jez! Oh, my goodness! Is it really you?"

He held her. "You're crying," he said.

"I'm just so happy to see you. What on earth are you doing here?"

"I came to see you."

"*Me?*"

"Of course."

"Oh, I feel so special."

"Well, you should feel so special. I'm a very busy man."

He set her down.

She kept her arms around him.

"Does Grandpapa know?" she said.

Grandpapa stood in the doorway, leaned against the wall. "Of course I know. I picked him up at the airport."

"Jez." She snapped her finger over his lips. "What on earth are you thinking? I'm coming back to America in, like, less than three weeks."

"I know. I missed you."

"But Jez. Tickets are *expensive*."

"Don't worry about that. Aren't you happy to see me?"

"Of course!"

"Okay."

"I'm *so* happy. I'm endlessly happy."

"Okay. Well, I'm here, then. Let's be happy."

His week in London was as happy as any of their time together.

His week in London was one of the last happy weeks they ever had together.

Two weeks after Jez returned to America, Lenore followed behind him for her second year at Harvard. They enjoyed one blissful week together—gathering up the pieces they had left behind in the spring, piecing them back together and sinking into their old routine. And then...

Jez received a phone call from Mr. Robert Darcy—personal assistant to the big boss, Mr. Charles Montana.

Mr. Montana requested Jez's presence at a private lunch in New Haven. Jez drove down there on noon of the following Monday, and Lenore wished him luck.

In case you couldn't guess, the lunch with Mr. Montana went well. Went *too* well, as it turned out.

Of course, at the time...

"Hey, pretty girl."

"Hey! Is the lunch over?"

"Yeah, yeah it is. I'm driving back right now."

"Oooh, how'd it go!"

"What are we doing tonight? Do you want to go to dinner?"

"Jez!"

"What?"

"Stop it, Jez! Tell me about your meeting."

It's funny how there are things in our lives, things that happen and we mark them mentally because we know they're monumental. Things that make a difference as far as the path we're on, that shift our lives like tectonic plates so that things are never again the same. I had a lot of moments like that in Nantucket, but the funny thing about those moments is we never realize *How Much*.

How Much of an impact those moments will actually have.

How Much the ripples will spread like fire.

How Much things will change.

It's funny.

How Much.

"Get this," Jez told Lenore that night at dinner. "They want to transfer me to Europe."

"Oh."

"What?"

"Europe, that's awesome."

"Lenore?"

"Yes?"

"It's a huge step for my career."

"No, I know."

"It's a huge opportunity."

But oh—

But oops—when rain falls in one place, another place is dry.

Lenore and Jez were left with less than three weeks together, then he settled into a new lifestyle in which he headed up the foreign division of a multimillion-dollar company. He hopped from historic city to historic city. He met with millionaires and billionaires from all over the world.

Jez attempted to maintain contact with Lenore after the move, but she was hurt, and he was busy, and time-zone conflicts limited their interaction to its narrowest flow in ages. They talked less often, less often. Their canal of shared waters bottlenecked. Nothing in their lives engendered or even fostered the depth and the breadth and the torrential current to which they had both become accustomed.

On the afternoon of October 27, 2004, Lenore and Jez spoke on the phone for the first time in a week. They closed the conversation with a classic and categorical knock-down-drag-out.

Jez was not the same person anymore—that's what Lenore told him.

Lenore was being obtuse and selfish—that's what Jez said.

Why couldn't he be back home in the States?

Why couldn't she just be happy for him that he was doing so well?

Jez, come back home, there are more important things than Career.

Lenore, life is not perfect, this is the real world.

She tried to tell Jez: Montana Inc. is robbing you of perspective.

He tried to tell Lenore: You don't understand.

That night the Red Sox won the World Series, and as fortuitously as things can go in life, Lenore met Maxwell Montana.

She and Jez began to drift from each other like boats with no anchors or sails.

Her plan to steal back his attention failed.

His plan to wait for her yielded no fruit.

Time passed, and nothing happened.

In the summer of 2006, Jez returned to the States, and two weeks later he received a Save The Date. The groom was to be Mr. Charles Montana Jr.

The bride was Miss Lenore Watson.

Jez broke three china plates and one drinking glass in his frustration, and he went to work on Monday and requested a transfer—away from Boston—to the Providence, Rhode Island branch of Montana Inc.

* * *

Sailboats dotted the Atlantic like white dots of liberty. The sun sparkled on the water. Jez stood beside Mr. Montana, in front of the mammoth window in Mr. Montana's Providence office, and the whole world looked like nothing but just one more of the man's possessions.

"You're sure you don't mind?" Mr. Montana asked.

"Sir, I am more than happy to go."

"Jez, I don't want you to think you have to. You know, you can take a bit of a break from work sometimes."

"Seriously, sir. I want to take this account."

"Best employee I have," Mr. Montana said. He put his hand on Jez's shoulder. "Best employee I have." They both kept looking out the window.

"Thank you, sir."

"Thank *you*. We'll go out to dinner after you return."

"Of course."

"I'll tell you all about the wedding," Mr. Montana said.

"Yes, sir. I can't wait to hear about it."

"You're *sure* you don't mind missing the wedding?"

"I'm positive," Jez said.

"Boy," Mr. Montana said. He faced Jez at last, and he winked. "You ought to see this young lady my boy is marrying. Is she ever a stunner."

"Oh, yes. I'll bet."

"I'm sure you'll meet her sometime, Jez."

"Yes, sir. I'm sure I will."

A week later Jez left for Germany.

A week after that, Lenore and Chas were married.

"We hadn't spoken for seven months," Jez told me. He was sitting beside Lenore on the couch in the sitting room. "And we didn't speak again for seven more months after that."

"Longest we ever went without talking," she said.

I forced a smile. I nodded.

Lenore had been married to Chas for seven months when she and Jez ran into each other at the Montana's annual Nantucket New Year's Eve party. It was the first time Jez had ever seen Lenore and Chas together.

"Are you happy?"

"Jez."

"Lenore, I want you to tell me."

"Jez, don't do this."

"Are you happy?"

"I am."

"*Are* you?"

"Of course I am."

"Okay," he said. "That's all I needed to know."

"I wasn't happy," she told me. "But I didn't know it yet."

"She didn't," Jez said.

Both of them smiled.

Incidentally, that night was the same night Chas met Lily Wrentsom.

Lily had attended the party with her husband, Wilson—an employee of Montana Inc.—the two of them having received a perfunctory invite because Wilson had been named Employee of the Year for his particular division.

Picture Lily—young, pretty, relegated to pinching pennies because she had married too young.

Lily—at The Palace, awash in a storm of wealth and affluence.

Picture Chas—drunk.

Chas—perhaps beginning to understand that perhaps his wife didn't love him.

The two of them—those separately married unsatisfied pictures of imagined oppression and emotional moribundity—started flirting, and they sneaked away, and they romped through the sheets upstairs.

It's funny.

How Much.

After that night, Lenore and Jez continued their break from talking. They ran into each other here and there—it was pretty much impossible for them to *not* run into each other, with the Montana family tying the two of them so closely together—but they held their interaction to nothing but nods and stiff *Hellos*. Once, Lenore told me, the two of them shook hands. She remembers it distinctly. It was the only time their skin touched throughout that vast-stretching ocean of time.

* * *

This last June Mr. Montana grabbed Jez and took him to Nantucket for a day of resting, relaxing, and strategizing.

They walked through the front door of The Palace, and Lenore was standing in the kitchen.

"Lenore..." Jez said. "Hi, how are you?"

"Ah," Mr. Montana said, "so the two of you *have* met. Jez, you're out of town so often, I wasn't sure whether you'd had a chance to meet her."

"Hello, Jez."

"Hello. Hi," he said again, "how are you?"

"I'm doing well."

"What are you doing here?"

"I'm living out here. For the summer."

"Oh."

"Come now, Lenore," Mr. Montana said, "let's not bore our prize employee. Would you mind grabbing us a couple drinks, my dear."

"Oh." Her eyes held onto Jez's. "Oh," she said again. "Certainly. What would you like to drink?"

"Jez, what would you like, son?"

"I—I'm fine."

"No, no, I insist. What'll you have to drink?"

"A water."

"Get me a bourbon," he said to Lenore, "on the rocks. And one for him as well."

Jez felt numb—his whole body. Like it wasn't even there. Everything felt displaced, out of order.

He sat in the drawing room with Mr. Montana. The sun chugged upward—progressing from the bottom of the window to the middle to the top—and all morning long, Mr. Montana talked.

Sometimes, Jez sipped his drink.

Sometimes, Jez chimed in.

His contributions contributed nothing.

In the afternoon, Mr. Montana excused himself with apologies. He needed some time with his financial volumes in the library.

"You can join me if you would like—there are some things I just need to study."

"Oh, that's fine—I'll stay out here."

"You're sure, Jez? You know that you don't have to."

"I'm sure, I'll be fine. I'll, um . . . I'll maybe take a walk. Down the beach."

"It's a beautiful beach."

"Yes."

"It's such a great house, isn't it? We don't get enough use out of it, son—to be perfectly honest. Yes, go take a walk on the beach, Jez. Go enjoy this beauty."

Jez stepped outside, and Lenore followed behind him.

They walked along the shoreline. They sat. They probably used one of the exact spots that I had used over the last few days.

"What are you doing out here?" he said to her. He whispered the words just loudly enough for them to carry over the surf.

"What do you mean?" she said.

He said nothing.

She continued. "I'm just taking some 'me' time, Jez. I . . . you know. I sit outside and work on my paintings. Enjoy the fresh air. It's absolutely lovely here."

"Lenore?"

"Jez."

"What are you doing out here?"

"I just told you."

Silence.

"What do you want me to say?" she said. "That I'm not happy? That things are awful? That everything is falling apart?"

"Do you know about Chas?"

"What about him?"

"Lenore . . . "

"Yes," she said. "Yes, okay. Yeah, I do know." The waves crashed, steady and persistent.

"Why are you putting yourself through this?"

"Do you know her name?"

"You're better than this, Lenore."

"I know."

"I do know her name."

"You do?"

"I've met her before."

"What is she like?"

"She's nothing. Absolutely nothing. Compared to you, at least."

"That's sweet of you to say."

"Do you really want to know her name?"

"Huh? No. Not really."

"No, I didn't think so."

A week and a half later he called Lenore from Providence. It was the first time he had called her in almost two years.

"Oh. Hello, Jez."

"It's June 16th."

"Yes?"

"Well ... " he said.

"Oh."

"I'm sorry," he said. "Should I not have called?"

"No. No, Jez. I'm happy that you did."

They started talking.

She started crying.

"Jez?"

"Yes."

"I can't believe you remembered."

"Really?"

"Yes. That's all."

"Why wouldn't I remember?"

"I don't know."

"Lenore, of *course* I remembered."

"Chas never remembers."

"Well. Lenore—"

"Chas didn't even call to wish me a happy birthday."

"Lenore."

"Yes?"

"Chas wasn't there when it happened. Chas wasn't there to help you make it through that. That's why he doesn't think about it."

"But you *were* there."

"Well. Yes. I was."

"You always are."

She stopped crying.

They talked for a while longer.

By the time Lenore hung up, she had nearly forgotten that her parents had died, six years earlier, on that exact date.

By the time Jez hung up, he was smiling.

I'm glad I called her, he thought. She needed that, I think. She needed to have my comfort . . .

. . . Yes, he thought, I've been here for her always.

* * *

The day was cloudy outside of the mammoth window in Mr. Montana's Providence office. The sailboats were missing. The ocean was gray. Jez stood across the desk from Mr. Montana, and Mr. Montana looked like he'd just been hit by a train.

"You say you need a *break*?" Mr. Montana said.

"Yes, sir."

"Well. That's not like you, Jez."

"I know, sir."

Mr. Montana stood. He turned to face the window, and he stayed like that for a while. He held his hands together behind his back. He spoke toward the window. "I like it," he said.

"You do?"

"I think you need a break, Jez. You work too damn hard."

"Thank you, sir."

He turned and looked at Jez again. "Of course. Work Monday, work Tuesday. Take the rest of the week off."

Jez arrived in Nantucket on Tuesday night. Lenore picked him up from the ferry and drove him to The Palace.

"We didn't sleep together," Jez told me.

"Not at first," she said.

"Not that week."

"You're right. Not that week."

"Not until the next time I came out here."

"We did kiss, though—that first week."

"True."

"And we did share a bed."

Jez laughed. "Also true. But we didn't sleep together."

"We didn't," she said.

Jez looked at me. "You at least have to give us credit for that."

Lenore said: "That's more courtesy than Chas ever showed."

"Lenore."

"Yes?"

"Cut Chas some slack."

"Why should I, Jez?"

"Because. It's just the way he is."

"You're right. You're probably right."

"Of course I'm right."

"You always are . . . "

They smiled at each other. I watched them. I waited for them to remember that I was also in the room.

I waited for them to continue their story . . .

Jez stayed with Lenore on Nantucket that week until Friday, and over the solitude and the beauty of those three days they rekindled the flame of their long-lost relationship. It was a relationship that broke the bounds of reality, that filled them both with the unbridled enthusiasm of an unrecoverable world at last discovered again.

The mornings were taken with breakfast and stories and laughing. The afternoons they reserved for relaxing—usually outside, by the ocean, beneath the unobtruded sky. The evenings were for reading, and the nights they saved for 'them'—a time when the two of them could cuddle and talk and occasionally kiss, just like the days of a once-forgotten past.

"How did I ever let you get away?" he would say to her.

"How did you ever *leave*?"

Jez returned to work the next Monday, July 21.

One week later, he escaped to Nantucket again.

"Another break from work?"

"Just one day, Mr. Montana."

"Which day?"

"Tuesday."

"What is that?"

"The 29th."

"What day is our meeting with the Japanese investors?" he asked.

"Wednesday."

"You'll be ready for it?"

"Of course."

"Okay..." Mr. Montana said.

"Okay?"

"You sure you're okay?"

"I'm sure."

"You just need a break?"

"I just need a break."

"Well. Okay," he said.

Jez said: "Okay."

Jez sneaked out to Nantucket again.

He stayed there Monday night and all day Tuesday.

Lenore and Jez slept together at last. For the first time ever. Consummating everything the two of them had been working toward together for so many years.

"We didn't plan it," she told me. "It just..."

" ... sort of happened," he said.

They both smiled.

"Sort of happened," she said. "Yeah."

"It was magical," Jez said.

"It really was."

"It was the most incredible experience I've ever had."

"It really was remarkable."

"But things got funny after that," he said.

"He's right," she said. "They did."

A week after Lenore and Jez slept together Jez tried to come to Nantucket once more.

Lenore would not allow him.

"You really don't want me to come out there?"

"I want you to. Of *course* I want you to."

"Why won't you let me?"

"Jez ... "

"Lenore."

"I just don't think it's ... "

"What?"

"I don't think it's right."

"Yeah?"

"What do *you* think?"

He thought she deserved happiness. He thought she should allow herself a tiny bit of sunshine. He thought Chas treated her awful, and he thought she deserved better.

He didn't tell her what he thought.

"I think you're probably right," he told her.

"I really wish I wasn't."

"I wish you weren't too."

"I just ... I feel so *awful*."

"I understand."

"I mean. Jez. I'm *cheating* on my husband."

"I know."

"That's not the kind of woman I want to be."

"I know."

He's cheating on you, Jez thought.

He didn't say this either.

What he said was: "We'll give it some time."

Lenore agreed. They would give it some time.

During this time, they began talking again—every single weekday.

During the weekends, Chas traveled to Nantucket out of marital obligation and put in his time with Lenore.

During the weekends, Jez passed the hours thinking about Lenore and imagining the future that they would someday, somehow, share with one another.

For the most part Chas ignored Lenore.

For the most part Jez ignored reality and instead explored a dreamworld inhabited by him and his one true love.

On November 21—the same day I flew into New England and stayed with Sandy and Shannon and her husband just outside the city, only one day before I went to Boston and met Maxwell and climbed on the roller coaster that comprised the next several weeks of my life—Lenore left for London.

"I was looking forward to spending time with you," Jez told her, a week before she left.

"Spending time with me when? *Where*?"

"In Nantucket. Over Thanksgiving. I can't believe you're leaving."

"Jez."

"Yes?"

"Chas will be there over Thanksgiving."

"I know that."

"The entire Montana *family* will be there over Thanksgiving."

"Lenore, I know that."

"How would we spend time together?"

"We could have made it happen."

"It wouldn't work. My goodness, Jez, I'm a married woman."

"Hardly."

"*Hardly?*"

"Look at the man you're married to."

"Jez—"

"Look at how he *treats* you, Lenore."

"Jez, don't yell."

"Lenore—"

"We can't keep doing this," she said.

"Lenore."

"Yes?"

"I love you."

"I know you do."

"I love you."

"I know."

"Are . . . are you sure you know?"

"Yes."

"Okay," he said.

"Okay," Lenore said.

They said nothing more.

* * *

Lenore jogged up the jetway, hoping she might catch her grandfather in time.

"Come on, come on," she said into her phone. "Come on, pick up."

"Hello?"

"Grandpapa!"

"You're not on your plane yet? My, I—"

"Grandpapa, I need you to turn around."

"Whoa, sweetie, what's—"

"I left something in the car, in the backseat, and I need it before I go."

"Sweetheart, I'm already at home."

"Grandpapa, please."

"What is it?"

"Huh?"

"What did you leave, dear? In the car?"

"Oh, I . . . something. Nothing. Please, Grandpapa, can't you make it back?"

"I'll mail it to you, sweetheart. There isn't any reason for me to trek back to the airport. Why, it would take me so long, and there's—"

"There's no reason for me to get on my flight unless I have it. Please, Grandpapa, if you make it back here quickly I can grab it and be on my flight in time."

"It's that important?"

"It is."

"I'll be there in fifteen minutes."

Lenore left the gate area and waited by the curb with her sweater gathered around her and her sundress blowing in the breeze. Her legs were cold. The time passed. Grandpapa's car jerked to the curb, and Lenore lunged toward him.

"Oh, Grandpapa, thank you!"

"You're welcome."

"You didn't look in the bag, did you?"

"Of course not."

"You're the best!"

"I know."

"Good-bye!" she called, and she ran back inside.

She pulled her phone out and called him again, twenty minutes later.

"*Grandpapaaaa.*"

"What's wrong, sweetheart?"

"I missed my flight!"

"You did, huh? How did that happen?"

"I did the best I could."

"Of course you did."

"By the time I made it through security again . . . well, I ran to my gate, but I was too late. Oh, I'm sorry, Grandpapa. Don't come back to get me, I'll just get a taxicab."

"No, no, dear. I—"

"No, don't drive back here."

"I won't drive back. I never left, I'll pick you up at the curb."

"You never left?"

"I didn't think you'd make your flight. No worries, I'm waiting for you out front. We'll reschedule your flight, okay? Reschedule it for tomorrow."

"Thank you, Grandpapa."

They both hung up, and she kept her phone open and dialed a new number.

"Awful news for you," she said. Walking through the airport. Future disaster behind her. Imminent mystery perched on her horizon.

"Awful news?" the man on the other end said.

"I didn't make my flight."

"Oh. That *is* awful news."

"I know." Both of them laughed.

"How did you manage that?"

"Well. I was on the plane already—I was pretty early, you would have been impressed with me—but just as I was finding my seat I realized that I had forgotten something, and I ran off the plane and called Grandpapa and made him come back."

"You *what*? How far away was he?"

"Back home."

"Back *home*? You made him come all the way back to the airport?"

"It was something rather important—so . . . he came back to bring it to me."

"Nothing is *that* important."

"It was a present for you."

"Oh," he said. "Really?"

"Really."

"Well, then. I guess that makes it worth it."

She and Jez talked some more. She reached her grandfather's car.

She and Grandpapa were headed to the market when the news of the plane crash crackled over the radio.

So close to death. So damn *close*.

Jez and Grandpapa were the only two people who knew that she'd left the flight.

Jez and Grandpapa were the only two people who knew that Lenore was alive.

CHAPTER 7

Late afternoon—

I sat by the ocean and threw rocks at the water.

Cecilia sneaked up behind me, and she lowered herself into the sand.

She sat beside me. She waited to speak. The wind that rushed off the water felt like ice.

"Are you okay?" she said, finally.

"I'm fine," I said.

"What's wrong?"

"I just told you, Cecilia. I'm fine."

"Okay."

She picked up a rock and threw it. It hit a wave and sunk and disappeared beneath the surface. She picked up another one.

"My parents were sure crazy at breakfast this morning."

"Yeah."

"Chas is taking this pretty hard."

I nodded.

"Have you seen Jez?"

Before I could answer—before I could bounce my voice off a springboard and yell, 'Yes, I *have* seen him! He's been next door all morning, in Sandy's house, talking to Lenore and telling me the entire sad history of the Jez and Lenore Saga. Yes, I've seen him—I've seen nothing *but* him—and he loves your brother's wife, and she's still alive, and they planned this all together!'— she started talking again:

"No one has seen him all morning. I wonder where he is."

"Yeah. I wonder too."

Nothing. No words. Both of us waited.

She threw her rock. It made a minimal splash and sunk and disappeared.

Cecilia stood, and she returned to The Palace.

I marvel, to look back and realize how much happened in those final 36 hours—in that day and a half that led to The End. A lifetime passed us all. A lifetime of secrets. A lifetime of tragedy. A lifetime of change.

Honesty. If only we'd all been honest with each other.

But isn't that the way things go? Isn't that life?

I returned to Banucci Manor sometime in the afternoon, and neither Lenore nor Jez was there. I stumbled through the house, looking for them both.

Inside of the house, the afternoon felt cold and searing.

Somewhere,

an open window.

Somewhere,

an open box of long-bottled feelings, finally released to the world.

I climbed the stairs and reached the bedroom in which Lenore was staying.

The open window in there. Sheets all rumpled.

I stood in the doorway and stared at the bed.

What happened in here?

Lenore and Jez had the house to themselves after I went away.

What happened?

I entered the room. With trepidation. I felt bad doing this—I felt awful snooping around like this—but feeling awful made no difference, because I continued to snoop.

Lenore's only possessions were stuffed into a small tote bag she had carried onto the plane with her, when she flew into the States in the private plane that Grandpapa had arranged. I reached into the bag and dragged out a garment. It still had the tag on it. I grabbed another one. The tag on this one as well. Clothes she had purchased before she came back here.

Her actual bags of luggage had crashed into the Atlantic and sunk beneath the surface and disappeared forever.

I grabbed a pair of jeans. No tag on these. I pulled them out from the bag.

Something fell from the folds of the legs and clattered across the floor.

I bent over and picked it up.

Small. Wooden.

I held it by my face.

It was a miniature punt boat. It had a pole tied to a string at the front. The pole was cracked down the middle.

In the floor of the boat there was a small loop of twine, only just large enough for me to slip my pinky into. I slipped my pinky into and pulled, and the bottom popped up.

Inside of this storage compartment, bedded down amongst tiny walls of red velvet, rested a small, folded piece of elaborate stationary.

I felt the paper. It felt like dried flowers.

I unfolded the paper and flipped it over, and printed—in a lovely, calligraphic hand—was a short, simple poem. I held it to the sunlight. The sunlight shone through the window and the paper.

"I love you," you said
I said, "I know"
"I love you," you said
"I know," I said
"Do you?" you said
"I do"
"Okay"
"Okay," I said
"Yes, okay"
But the days are wasted
When you're away
I sit alone
I wish and pray
I want to return
I need to say
I love you, Jez
I love you, I do
I love you
I love you
It's all okay

I stared at the paper.

Oh my goodness . . .

I stared at the paper.

The present for Jez . . .

I stared at the paper. I trailed my fingers across it.

Oh my goodness, the present for Jez. The reason Lenore was still alive.

I love you, it said.

It's all okay.

I folded the note, just as I had found it, and I placed it in the floor of the punt. I lowered the lid. I wrapped the small wooden souvenir into the legs of her jeans, and I placed the jeans in the bag. I placed her clothes in the bag. I rumpled everything up, just a little bit, just like it had been before. I left the room and walked downstairs and left the house, and I trailed along the beach.

At some point out there—maybe after I'd been walking along the beach for a few minutes, or maybe after I'd been walking out there for a very long time—I ran into Maxwell. He was walking along the beach also. He looked weary. Overwhelmed. He waved to me and we started walking together and neither of us spoke.

Maxwell walked faster than me, and I tried to keep up. Both of us left behind us a tempest of merging but unshared secrets and pains.

"Let's go walk on the road," he said. He had stopped. He was facing me.

"What's on the road?"

"Nothing."

"Okay."

He started walking again. "We'll walk out near the point. It isn't far."

"Okay," I said again.

"I just need a change of scene."

"I understand you there."

"This is starting to be too much, brother. I'm ready for all of this to end."

"How do you mean?"

Maxwell left the sand and cut through the grass and headed toward the road. "I mean I'm ready for the damn memorial service tomorrow so we can finally lay Lenore to rest, and move on with our lives. I'm ready to get back to my apartment and get drunk and forget everything."

"You're drunk right now."

"Yup. But I haven't forgotten everything."

The grass crunched underneath us. The sky looked clear and cheery, mocking Maxwell and me and the swirling darkness that engulfed us both.

A couple minutes later the two of us reached the road. It swept away around a bend littered sparingly with long-dead leaves and stray specks of sand, like billboards announcing that this vacation destination had closed for the winter.

Other than the smattering of families who stayed on the island year-round—most of whom lived further inland—the island was pretty much empty. The raucous laughter and pictures and memory-making of warmer months all disappeared during this time of year, and cold swept in, and the island hibernated. And Maxwell and I were the lone travelers walking the road on this blustery day in the middle of December.

If we traveled inland we would find the quaint town of Nantucket twinkling in Christmas lights, but where we were— on the outskirts of the world—all was barren and empty. All was close to dead.

The road gave off cold like a mist that permeated my shoes and made my feet shiver. The cold climbed my legs. Reached my knees. Trickled up higher. Maxwell and I kept walking, and neither of us carried a single thing worth saying. We thought the same thoughts, and we drifted further apart.

When Maxwell and I reached the entrance to the point, he left the road and forged a path through the tall, swaying grass. He crunched out onto the sand. I followed him. We reached the water, and we stood there for maybe ten seconds before Maxwell turned around.

"Where are you going?"

"Back."

"Already?"

He didn't answer. I didn't say anything else. I let him walk away, and I gathered my coat around me and watched the cold, restless, ever-shifting Atlantic.

* * *

So many elements go into the assemblage of a story.

As a writer I have found that you don't so much Create a story as Discover, uncovering bit-by-bit the different parts that allow the whole to come together. It's as though an armload of unrelated components are dropped into a boiling cauldron, and in the end—after everything mellows and stews and meshes together for enough minutes—a finished product pops out. Something you could never have created on your own.

I am beginning to realize that there will *be* no second great novel from the fingertips of Richard Parkland. Not for a while, at least. I spent weeks on Nantucket, trying to begin, but nothing arose from all those hours of work, and now I've spent weeks upon weeks in Paris. Pounding my head against the wall. Trying to free up some sort of creative flow. And still, nothing.

To pass the time I have clicked away on the keyboard composing this memoir of those fateful Nantucket weeks, and I feel right now as though there is no way for me to continue with my writing career at all until I record and rationalize everything that happened. How everything came together. How the components in my life—and the lives of those around me—were dropped into a cauldron and boiled together until The End was achieved.

That is one thing I love about writing. About literature. About stories. The End.

Oh yeah.

All right.

Are you gonna be in my dreams tonight?

But in real life, there is no The End. There is no tidy conclusion all wrapped in a package, with a bow tied around it.

In real life, life goes on. It's all so messy.

I gaze back over the experiences behind me (almost like I'm gazing over a landscape filled with fields and mountains and streams and trees), and I see how perfectly everything fit. I see how "coincidences" corresponded with life, and how life progressed, and how everything had to happen exactly how it happened, and *How Much*.

How Much.

Then I stop thinking. I sit at my desk and pour a glass of whiskey, and I try to start writing.

It's the only way to forget.

It's the only way to move forward.

It's the only medicine I have.

* * *

I finally left the water and returned to the road. The cold made it feel like I'd been out there for hours, but it was probably no longer than maybe two or three minutes.

The road dipped and bent away from me where I walked. I watched a leaf tumble over the blacktop. I rounded the bend and started approaching the houses, and I stopped.

My mind labored, dragged—but my feet started moving. My legs pumped as they reacted to what my eyes saw. I raced toward the car.

"Stop!" I yelled.

"Get off me!"

"Stop!" I yelled again.

"Get off me!" she yelled again.

I caught Maxwell with my shoulder, and I peeled him off her, and I slammed him against the car. He used my momentum to keep me moving, flinging me off him. He lunged at the girl again.

"Help me!" she yelled.

I lost my balance and rolled off the back of the car and pummeled the ground. My shoulder jarred itself into my body.

"Listen to me," Maxwell yelled. "Listen!"

"Get off her!"

"Help me, get him off me!"

"Get off her!" I yelled again. I grabbed the back of the car and pulled my feet under me and charged.

The girl screamed.

I twisted Maxwell around.

Maxwell swung, and he caught me in the jaw.

Moments. Passing.

Pain.

I stumbled backward.

"Sorry," Maxwell said. He tugged at the bottom of his shirt. "Sorry."

"Oh my *God*, Maxwell," the girl said. "Stop going so *crazy*."

I regained my balance. I rubbed my jaw.

"Sorry," he said again. "You okay?"

"Yeah," I said to Maxwell. "Yeah, I'm okay." I looked at the girl. She looked at me. She looked familiar. "Who . . . ?"

"This is Lily."

"Ah," I said. I nodded. I leaned forward and reached for her hand. "Lily. Of course. A pleasure to meet you."

* * *

The three of us stood in the road beside the car saying pointless things for about a minute.

Maxwell stood across from Lily. I stood beside them both.

"She almost hit me," Maxwell told me.

"I didn't almost hit you."

"You *did*. With her car," he told me. He pointed at her car—a bright yellow spectacle of metal and rubber and glass.

"I'm a careful driver," she said.

"Maybe. But you still almost hit me."

"I wouldn't hit someone unless I meant to."

"Maybe you meant to."

"Why would I mean to hit you?"

"You wouldn't. I was just saying."

"I didn't almost hit him," she said to me.

"Okay," I said.

Maxwell had been almost back to The Palace when Lily almost hit him. She was careening down the road in a fury of anger and unrestrained hatred—on her way to The Palace herself—when she swerved away from Maxwell and hopped out of the car to make sure he was okay.

"Oh," she said, "oh, I'm so sorry! I almost hit you, are you okay! I—Max. Oh, I didn't know that was you."

"I'm okay."

"I'm sorry."

"I'm fine, really. Lil, what are you doing here?"

"I . . ."

"Lil?"

She ran back to the car.

"Lil!"

She opened the door and tried to climb inside and Maxwell grabbed the back of her arms and yanked her away. He slammed the door shut.

"Stop it! Get off me, Max!"

"Lil, listen."

"Get off me!"

"Listen to me, Lil. You don't want to do this."

She stopped moving. She stopped fighting. He let go of her arms.

"Lil, this isn't going to make things better. Okay? Calm down for a moment and think about all this. You don't want to do anything that you'll regret later." He waited for her to answer, but she didn't. He continued. "Just breathe, Lil. You don't want to do this. It's all okay."

"Jez called me."

"He what?"

"He called me."

"What did he say?"

Lily was crying. "He told me that Lenore was dead."

"She is."

"And he—oh, Max."

"You're okay, Lil. You're okay."

"He told me that Chas is heartbroken. He told me that Chas hasn't stopped crying in days, and that Chas wants nothing more than a second chance with Lenore. That Chas still [*sob!*] loves her, he said, oh, Max."

"You're okay, Lil. You're okay."

She hit the car with her palms. She cried harder. She tried to run toward the house.

That's when I had rounded the bend, and had seen Maxwell grabbing her, and had seen him fighting to force her back against the car.

She calmed down a bit, after I got there and got punched by Maxwell and met her. She breathed more normal, and she sounded sane when she talked.

"I love him," she said. She sat on the hood of the car and cried so hard that the tears dripped off her face and landed on her jeans. "I love him so damn *much*."

Maxwell's hands rested on her thighs.

I stood to the side and watched them.

"Shhh. I know you do, Lil. I know."

"I do. And he told me that he loves me, Max. He *told* me that. He hates me now."

"He doesn't hate you."

"I tried to call him. Twelve times I tried. He wouldn't pick up my phone calls."

"He's having a rough time with all this."

"*Why!*"

"What?"

"He *told* me he didn't love her! He told me he *hated* her. All the time he told me, Max. All the *time!*"

"Whoa, Lil—"

"All the time! And he would say he just wanted to escape from her and move on with his life, he said that marrying her was the biggest mistake ever. That's what he said!"

"Stop it, Lil."

"He did."

"I don't want to hear that."

"We slept together all summer."

"Lil!"

"What do you want me to say! All summer, Max. I slept in *her* bed. I used *her* house. I cooked in *her* kitchen and lived with *her* husband. All *sum*mer! She abandoned him, Maxwell. She moved to Nantucket for the summer, because she didn't love him either. And I lived with him, and *she—never—knew.*"

"You're not making things better, Lil."

"I love him."

"I know you do."

"And I hate her!"

"She's dead."

"She's ruining my life ..."

"Calm down, all right? It's all gonna work out in the end."

"Max," she said. She paused. She looked at him more closely. "Max, have you been drinking?"

"No. Yes. Why?"

"You're never so optimistic unless you've been drinking."

"I'm just trying to help."

"I know you are."

Her sobs were slowing down. Her everything was slowing down. The tornadic potential of Lily On The Island And Heading To The Palace was beginning to slowly abate. Maxwell kept his hands on her thighs and she kept her hands near her face, and I kept watching.

"But . . . Maxwell?"

"Yeah?"

"But . . . why won't he return my phone calls?"

"Because," Maxwell said.

"Because?"

"Because," he said. "He doesn't love you anymore."

She looked up. She looked at Maxwell's face. "Stop it."

"He doesn't."

"Stop it!"

"He told me. He told Jez. He doesn't love you anymore."

"*Stop*itstopitstopit—" crying all over again.

"He told anyone who would listen, Lily." Maxwell was talking louder now. "He loves Lenore, and he wants you out of his life."

She bent over. Kept crying. "*Stop*itstopitstopit." She jumped off the hood and ran toward the house, and we both lunged to grab her.

* * *

"Maxwell?"

"Rich."

"Did he really say that?"

"Who?"

"Chas."

"Did he really say what?"

"You know what I'm talking about."

"No," Maxwell said. He sighed. "No, brother. He didn't."

"Then why did you tell her that?"

"Huh?"

"Lily," I said. "Why did you tell her that he said that?"

Maxwell turned the wheel and pulled into the driveway.

We had just finished escorting Lily to the ferry, and neither of us had spoken until now.

"What do you want me to say, huh? What was I supposed to do, Richard? Lily loves my brother."

"Does he love her?"

"Of course he does . . . you know, in his own way."

"I don't understand."

He pulled up alongside the house. Put the car in park. Removed the keys and leaned his head back and took a deep breath. "It isn't right."

"I know."

"Lenore deserves better."

"I know."

"You would understand if you'd met her, Richard. It's just . . . I just . . . think that it'd be best—for everyone—if Lily stayed away from my brother. It would keep him from desecrating the memory of Lenore by screwing around on her during the mourning period. It would keep Lily from getting hurt again. It would. It will . . . it will lessen the drama so damn much."

And there it was. Those last words. A premonition of the awfulness to come. A foreshadowing of the day and a half ahead of us. A sign . . .

How Much.

Of how much shit we still had left to go through.

If only we'd known at the time. We might have done things differently.

Maxwell gazed across the grass toward the beauty of Banucci Manor and opened the car door and started to climb out. "Let's go over to Sandy's house," he said.

I gazed in the same direction and opened the door and started to climb out also. I pictured Lenore and Jez, inside of Banucci Manor, in the upstairs bedroom. "Let's go out to the beach."

"The beach? It's freezing."

"I know."

"I think it's about to snow."

"I think so too."

"Okay," he said. "Sure. Let's go out to the beach."

Not long after that the snow slapped us and stung our skin. We walked briskly, trying to shield our faces.

I peered out from a narrow slit between my coat and my hat, and Maxwell looked at me and chuckled.

It was one of the only genuine smiles I had seen all week.

We had almost reached The Palace when we noticed Jez. He was jogging across the lawn.

"Is that Jez?" Maxwell asked. It was a rhetorical question.

I answered anyway. "It is."

"What is he doing?"

"No telling."

"What's that he's got in his hand?"

We had both stopped walking. The snow pelted us. "That's a punt boat."

"A what?"

"A miniature punt boat."

"What's he have that for?"

"Nothing," I said. "Absolutely nothing."

Neither of us moved. I don't know why.

Jez disappeared around the corner of Banucci Manor, then he reappeared a few moments later.

The punt boat was gone.

I noticed this, even if Maxwell didn't. I noticed because I knew what was in there.

Secret notes. Passing back and fo—

"I'm gonna kill him."

"Maxwell, whoa—" but he had already lowered his head and started marching toward Sandy's house. "Maxwell, hold on a minute. Hold on, man."

"Maxwell, hey," Jez called. He raised a hand in genteel salutation.

Maxwell kept stomping forward.

Somewhere, time froze. I stood within the awful wake of anger, and I waited to see what would happen.

I freely admit it: Sometimes I am genuinely no help at all.

"Whoa, bud. You okay?" Jez said. These words floated and danced in the wind, and I heard them—but only just barely. I heard them—but only just as Maxwell swung.

It was a heavy blow, focused and unwavering. It met Jez's face, and Jez met the ground. Life burst through me, and I sprinted toward Maxwell.

Maxwell: "What kind of game are you playing!"

Me: "Stop it, Maxwell!"

Maxwell: "You're not a part of our family—you got that? And you never will be!"

Me: "Maxwell!"

"What are you saying?" Jez asked. He was sprawled across the grass. Snow attacked his body.

"What am I—what am I saying? What am I *say*—" he lunged down and grabbed the lapels of Jez's coat, "—*ing*! What do you *think* I'm *saying*!" he let go of the lapels, and Jez hit the ground. "You arrogant [*punch in the stomach*], goddamn [*punch in the stomach*], son of a [*punch in the stoma*—]"

"Maxwell!" I yelled, and I grabbed him and yanked him backward.

Tears covered his cheeks. He pushed me and pulled me toward him and held me for a second before pushing me again.

"What's wrong, Maxwell?"

"What is he thinking!"

"What's wrong?"

"He isn't part of our family! He doesn't know what this is *like*."

"You're all right, bud. Shhh—Maxwell, it's all okay."

"He hardly *knew* Lenore. He didn't know her. He doesn't know what this is like." He spun around and faced Jez and pointed with both his hands. "Why did you do it!"

Jez was standing again. One hand rubbed his face. "What are you even talking about?"

"Tell me right now, Jez, or I swear to God I'll come after you again."

"What is wrong with you, man? Richard, what's wrong with him?"

"Oh. Ohhh, what's wrong with me? There's plenty wrong with me, you *bitch*! Plenty right now, but I'm trying to take care of it a little bit at a goddamn time. First things first, Jez. Why the hell did you do it?"

"Do what?" Jez said. He looked at me. "Do what, Richard? Do you know what he's going on about?"

"Why did you call Lily."

"Oh."

"Yeah. Yeah, asshole. *Oh.*"

"I was only trying to help."

"Sonofa—"

I grabbed Maxwell and held him.

He shook his head. Spoke to Jez. "If you'd known her," he said. "If you'd gone through the things I've gone through. If you were having to go through the things I'm going through *right now*, you wouldn't be such a *bitch*."

"You don't know what you're saying."

"Oh, I *know*. You think you're so damn special—you think you're hot shit because you're smart, and 'cause my father likes you the most. I got news for you, though. That doesn't matter."

Jez shook his head. "Stop talking," he said.

"It doesn't matter one bit. You're not a part of this family. You have no right. *No damn right.* To try and involve yourself in things like this. My brother? His girlfriend? Look, *buddy.* I hate all of that as much as anyone. I disapprove of it more than *anyone.* But you have no damn right to meddle in my family. You have no right to try and screw with my family. If you do one more thing to cross us, I swear...I won't stop until I see you ruined. You understand *that*?"

They stared at each other. Neither man spoke.

The silence making me uncomfortable...

I cleared my throat, and both of them turned.

The words pulsing in my mouth, pushing their way out...

I fought to keep them down.

There was nothing I could do.

"Lenore is alive," I said, choking on the words.

"What?" Maxwell said. He leaned forward. He legitimately had not understood me.

Once again, fighting to quash the words...

Too late—

"She's alive. She's staying in Sandy's house. I..."

Somewhere, a clock ticked. Somewhere, time disappeared.

Somewhere,

Somewhere,

Somewhere.

"Jez and Lenore planned the whole thing together."

Maxwell looked at me. He looked at Jez. He stumbled backward and lost his feet and tumbled.

CHAPTER 8

I think of a book.

I think of the finished product—how we hold it and feel its texture while we dive within its pages. How we sometimes read a book in a single, exhilarating sitting.

For those of us whose lives are too busy to allow for single-sitting reads I think of how a book accompanies us on the subway, or how we keep it in our car. How we sit in bed at night and burn through the pages until we're ready to fall asleep. I think of that fortunate fraternity who is lucky enough to have found someone to love—how that someone lies beside you with their body curled and their eyes closed, saying, 'Darling, please, turn out that light. Please, I'm ready to fall asleep.' And how you say to them, 'Just one more section, sweetheart. Just one more chapter.' And your love sighs, and you rest your hand on their back, and you continue to turn the pages until you can't keep your eyes open one more minute.

I think of the manner in which we behold a book—the manner in which we behold any work of art, in fact, whether it be music or paintings or stories—how we explore and absorb and rejoice and enjoy, and how we so rarely stop, and so rarely think: What did it take to make this?

I have not touched this memoir for over two months.

Perhaps I tried to forget.

Perhaps I tried to trick myself into believing that I could move on with my life—move on with my writing—without ever resolving the past that weighs on me with such a heavy hand.

But ah, such is not the case.

There will be no second great novel poured forth from the once-luminous mind of Richard Parkland until I slog through the rest of this memoir. Until I create a place where I can insert The End.

The End will be hopeful.

The End will be imagined.

Four days ago I was sitting by the river and smoking a cigarette, staring at a high pale moon in the high pale afternoon blue, when I said to myself, "Richard, good sir, it isn't going to work."

"Yes," I said, "I know."

"Do you?"

"Of course."

"Your second novel . . . "

"Yes?"

"You'll never be able to write it until you first go back and close the book on the Nantucket portion of your life."

"I know," I said again, and I stood and looked around to see if anyone was listening to me, then I pulled my feet up and returned to my flat.

Four days later—here I am, trying once more to remember and resolve those terrible things that happened in my life four terrible months ago.

* * *

The church was white. It sat on top of a sloped lawn in the quaint little town of Winchester, Massachusetts, with a narrow park across from it and the cement wall of a train stop looming beyond that. A bell tolled above us, and we walked from the parking lot to the door of the church like a nighttime wave breaking onto the shore.

The ushers led Jez and me to a pew, three rows from the front. We scooted in and sat down with painted somber faces, and the two of us pretended we had not known Lenore on any level of remotely personal qualities. He and I also pretended that Lenore was dead. Of all the people filtering into the church and sitting down with mournful faces, Jez and I were the only ones with a clue.

He and I exchanged a glance. It was the sole acknowledgement between us, as neither of us had quite resolved our dispute from the previous afternoon...

"What the hell!" Jez had yelled.

Maxwell sat in the snow, sat where he had fallen after I told him Lenore was still alive.

"Maxwell," I said. I stepped forward. "Maxwell, bud—you okay?"

"Stay away from me."

"Maxwell?"

"What the hell!" Jez yelled again.

"Shut up, Jez! Maxwell—Maxwell, come on, bud."

"Stay away from me, brother."

Step forward.

"I said stay away. Stay away!"

"What are you playing at, Richard!"

"Shut up, Jez!"

Step forward.

Maxwell: scooting further away. "Stay away," he said—now nearly a whisper. "Stay away, brother. Ohhh, stay away."

And Maxwell was several feet removed from us—drag marks streaking through the snow, marking the spot from which he'd pulled himself along and forced himself to his feet.

"Stay away," he said again, and his words danced off with the wind. He stuck his head down and marched toward The Palace, and as he left our bubble of interaction I still heard him muttering: "Stay away, stay away, stayaway stayaway stayaway..."

"What the hell," Jez said, one final time.

And instead of following Maxwell I stared at Jez for a few long seconds before turning and tramping through the driving snow, toward the back door of Banucci Manor.

I'm going to show him, I thought. Oh, man, am I ever going to show him. Boy-oh-boy, he's taken things too far, and I'm sickandtired of it and it's time for all of this to come to light.

Jez hustled along beside me. He said things into my ear.

I kept walking, and I asked about the punt boat.

He told me it was no big deal.

"It's no big deal, really, just leave it all alone, okay? Richard—please, Rich, just calm down a little bit, take a moment to think. No need for anything brash, all right, you're jumping to conclusions." His words continued.

I continued.

I reached the back patio, and the punt boat wasn't there.

"—no big deal," I heard him say again, but my hand was already on the handle, and I was already pulling the door open and stomping inside.

Snow trailed behind me.

Jez trailed behind the snow.

Lenore stood in the living room with her hands on her hips. "Richard."

I stopped walking.

Jez caught up to me. He stopped walking also.

"Lenore," I said.

"Jez."

"Lenore."

"Sit down, you two."

We sat.

Lenore gazed through the window. Jez and I waited in silence, staring into separate points in the infinite forever.

She paced for a bit.

She returned her hands to her hips, and she returned her eyes to us.

"I'm disappointed in you both."

Her gaze pierced me. It felt like she and I were the only two people in the room.

I imagine that Jez felt the same way. I don't know for certain, because I never got a chance to ask him.

She left the room.

Jez and I continued to stare into separate points in the infinite forever, waiting for Lenore.

Somewhere, a clock ticked. Somewhere, time disappeared.

Somewhere, later in the night, the wind attacked me, and Maxwell reached into his pocket and pulled out a cigarette. He struggled to keep the lighter alive long enough to ignite, and when he finally got it rolling he took a puff and expelled the smoke and reached into his pocket again, searching for an extra smoke he could offer to me. It took him a couple moments and a few more puffs to realize that the one in his mouth was the last one on him, and he removed it, and he offered me a drag.

I waved him away.

He took another puff and expelled the smoke, and it disappeared behind him.

"Lenore's not gonna go to her funeral tomorrow."

"No?" I said.

"Yeah. She told me that a little bit ago."

"You went to see her, huh?"

"I did."

"I thought you said you weren't going to."

"Yeah. Well. I couldn't help myself, brother."

"I understand."

"I couldn't help myself."

"So . . . she's not going to her funeral, huh?"

"Yeah. She's gonna call her grandfather in the morning, and he's gonna arrange a private plane."

"Who's going to take her?"

"Take her?"

"To the plane."

"Oh—to the . . . yeah. I am."

"You're going to miss the funeral?"

"She's not really dead, you know?"

"I know."

Maxwell laughed a little. "Just checking," he said. He flicked the cigarette forward, and the wind flicked it behind us. He reached in his pocket once more, then he remembered that he was all out. "Things go okay with Cecilia?" he asked, pulling his hand out of his pocket and using it to scratch his face.

"No," I said, "not really."

"How so?"

"How did things go with Lenore?" I asked. I did not feel like discussing Cecilia.

"Things went okay."

"Yeah?"

"Things went okay . . . "

When Lenore returned to the living room several hours earlier—allowing Jez and me to tear our eyes away from our separate focused points in the infinite forever—she handed me an envelope. On the front of the envelope she had written Maxwell's name. She asked me to bring it to him, and I told her that he would not read it.

"He will."

"He won't," I said. "I guarantee it."

"Just take it to him, Richard. He will."

"— that," Maxwell said. He was sitting in the second floor living room of The Palace when I found him, staring at the windows. The sun was disappearing into the far-away continent behind us.

"Yeah?" I asked. I stood beside the couch and looked down at him. He looked lost. He looked old.

"Yeah," he said, "— that, Richy—I'm not gonna read it."

"That's what I told her."

"I'm *not.*"

"Okay."

"Sit down, brother, you're making me nervous."

"Sorry, sorry."

"Where's that envelope anyhow?"

"Right here."

"Let me see that."

"Sure." I handed him the envelope.

Maxwell stared at it for two or three seconds, and I realized that this envelope—his name printed across the front in Lenore's lovely, archaic handwriting—brought him closer to a concrete, breathing, alive Lenore than he had imagined he ever again would be.

He folded the envelope and shoved it into his pocket.

"She really is alive then, huh?"

"She really is alive."

"— that," he said again. "— Lenore. I'm not gonna read this."

Shortly after that, Maxwell entered Banucci Manor. Lenore met him in the living room.

"So," he said to her, and he shoved his hands into his pockets and did his best to relax his shoulders. "You're still alive, huh?"

"I'm still alive."

"*That's* pretty crazy."

"I know, right?"

"Wow," he said. His eyes joined hers, and they spent several indeterminable moments locked in a tenuous visual embrace.

"Aren't you going to give me a hug?" she said.

Maxwell crossed the valley of unreality between them and touched her outstretched hand—Live skin! Warm and alive!—and pulled her body toward him. They held each other. The ticking clocks and passing time no longer existed, and they wandered through a world several worlds removed from our own.

When they finally released each other she took his hand again and led him upstairs. They entered the sitting room, and the coffee table he had flipped over and shoved into the wall the previous evening still rested where he had left it, upside down, whispering discontent.

Maxwell spoke, and after no more than a handful of minutes they managed to drown out these whispers of discontent—and all other whispers besides—with their first candid, honest, and pleasant conversation in years.

"She asked me why I never dated her," he told me.

The wind had picked up.

"What did you say?"

"I told her I didn't know. I told her I didn't have a clue."

"Yeah?"

"I didn't, brother—*don't*. I don't have a clue. Think of how different things would be."

"That's the truth."

"All of this," he said. He swept his hand out toward the ocean, as if its wind-driven turbulence was a perfect portrayal of the picture in which our lives had become trapped. But he said nothing else.

"Why did she decide to skip her funeral?" I asked again.

"I told you," Maxwell said, "I don't really know. It's just sort of a decision she made—she just made it while we were talking."

"You think she'll follow through with it?"

"Of *course* she'll follow through with it."

"Okay."

"Why would you even *ask* that?"

"I don't know."

"Of *course* she'll follow through with it. But hey, tell me what happened with you and Cee."

"Oh," I said.

"Come on."

"Okay," I said.

If not for Cecilia, there is a chance that none of this would have happened.

Earlier in the night—

Knock knock knock.

Maxwell and I both turned around, and we watched the door as it opened a crack and opened a crack more and finally gave way to Cecilia's lovely face.

"It okay if I come in?"

"Of course," Maxwell said. We'd been sitting there for thirty minutes since I handed him the letter from Lenore—the two of us talking about things that neither of us will ever actually remember.

"Richard?" she said.

"Of course," I said, "come on in."

Cecilia pushed the door open a few more inches, and she squeezed through the doorway as if there was something on the other side that kept her from opening the door all the way.

"What's up?" I said.

"What are you guys up to?"

"We're just talking."

"Yeah?"

"What are you up to?" Maxwell asked. "You okay? You look a little pale."

"I always look a little pale."

Maxwell chuckled.

"The curse of the redhead."

Maxwell chuckled again.

Cecilia was wearing tight jeans and an extra-loose hooded sweatshirt—gray, with yellow writing. Her ponytail was even looser and less-contained than normal, and her contacts were out and her black-framed, square-framed eyeglasses were on. She looked beautiful, like a taste of hot life.

She stood in the doorway with her sleeves hanging down and covering her hands before she finally started fidgeting and finally cleared her throat and finally spoke up. Maxwell and I watched her, waiting for her words.

"Hey, um," she coughed. "Sorry. Haha. Oh," and she pushed her hair off her face. "Um," she said again, "do you think we can talk for a minute?"

"Me?"

Maxwell laughed—the first genuine laugh I'd heard from him in days. He grabbed his knee, then he punched my thigh. "Of course she means you."

Cecilia smiled. Her smile was strained.

"Yeah," I said, "um—yeah, sure. You *do* mean me, right?"

Cecilia nodded.

"Of course she means you," Maxwell said again. He grabbed his knee and punched my thigh. "It comes with the territory, brother."

And that's when I knew that I was in trouble.

If Cecilia had been in an okay mood she would have said something to Maxwell along these lines: 'The *ter*ritory?'

Something along the lines of, 'Hey, c'mon, I'm at least more than *ter*ritory.' When she only pursed her lips, however, and nodded and pushed her hair out of her face again instead of saying anything fun and playful, I knew I was in for a serious discussion.

"Sure," I said to Cecilia, averting my eyes. "Sure, we can talk. Right now?"

"If that's okay."

"Um...yeah." I looked at Maxwell. Maxwell nodded. "Sure," I said. "That's perfectly fine."

"Okay. Good. Thank you."

"You sure?" I said to Maxwell.

"Go for it, brother—I'm fine, right?"

"Okay," I said again. I followed Cecilia from the room.

* * *

Cecilia played with a rock and watched the water, and the wind tossed the stray strands of her hair this way and that.

I wanted to hold her. With her gorgeous face and lovely hair and inviting outfit, with her cute little glasses and fantastic body, I wanted to whisper into her ear and have her whisper back. I wanted to know that I'd made a mistake by shunting her aside over the last few days, to know that she was actually as amazing as she looked. I wanted her to think of me the same way I wanted to think of her.

Then, Cecilia spoke.

"Richard. What's wrong?"

"What?"

They were the first words she'd let fly since I followed her from the living room on the second floor of The Palace. We had walked across the grass and walked along the street, and we strode in silence for several minutes until we reached the entrance to the point where Maxwell and I had traveled earlier in the day, and we found a spot on the sand to sit. And that's when Cecilia asked me, Richard, what's wrong?

After I asked her What? she played with the rock some more before speaking again.

"Things have been weird, Richard. You've been acting weird."

"I haven't been acting weird."

"You have, Richard. You've been acting 'off.' "

"I know."

"Do you?"

"I do."

The moon danced on the surface of the water, painting a swath of the magnificent black a bottomless soft and mysterious silver.

"Why is it?" she asked.

"I don't know, Cecilia. I don't know. It's just, things have been going weird with my—"

"And please, baby—I have to ask you, above and beyond all else—please don't blame it on your writing. That's what you were going to say, isn't it?"

"Well—"

"It is, I know. Oh, I know—and I know that's a legitimate excuse. Hey, I'm not a creative person like you. I don't know how those things work, and maybe your offness is a byproduct of your, you know—of issues with your writing. But I just need something more concrete than that, Richard. You understand, don't you?"

"Sure. I understand."

"I don't know. Maybe I'm being nagging. Am I being nagging?"

"Cecilia—"

"I know I'm that way at times—Max is always telling me that: Cecilia, don't be so nagging, you're always so nagging—but sometimes I just can't help it. Richard, *am* I being nagging?"

"You're okay."

"I don't feel okay. I just wish I knew what I could do to make things less weird between us."

"I—"

"I really like you a lot, you know."

"I know."

"Hey, let's go into the shack." She stood, and I stood also, and I followed her deeper onto the point through the tall, rustling grass.

To be honest, I'm really not sure why the shack was there on the point in the first place. From what I understand it was built by an *Old Man and the Sea*-type fisherman sometime during the 1950s, and by the time anyone actually made any mention of tearing it down it had achieved a sort of sentimental value among a handful of the island's residents. Nothing was ever decided on the issue, and this was decision enough to allow the thing to stay standing until the wind itself saw fit to do the job.

If the shack was an eyesore (and certainly it was) it was a small eyesore, and most of those who visited the point were content to overlook it, or even to see it as a charming addition to their charming pocket of the world.

Of greater relevance, no one ever really entered the shack. No one besides Cecilia and myself, on the night before the beginning of The End.

"Isn't this place fun?" she said. We sat side-by-side on the edge of the old bed, and when she decided to bounce a little bit to show me just how *fun* this place really was, mold and mildew and assorted nastiness leaped from the mattress and mixed with the air.

I coughed.

She bounced a bit more.

"Sure," I said. "Yeah, it's fun. Can you stop bouncing like that."

"Sure."

"Thank you."

"I wish you *weren't* so off, Richard. I wish I could do something to help."

"Yeah."

"*Is* there anything I can do?"

"I don't think so."

"Are you *sure*?"

"I don't know, Cecilia."

Cecilia started kissing me, and I grabbed her shoulders and pulled myself away.

"Cecilia," I said.

"Baby."

"Cecilia," I said, and she started to kiss me again.

She moved from my lips to my earlobe to my neck. She pulled my shirt up.

The night was cold.

She kissed my stomach.

She lied down on the bed, and she pulled me down with her.

I forgot about the nastiness jumping off the mattress, and I forgot about coughing, and I even forgot that I had just pulled her away and tried to make her stop.

Her hand touched my knee.

Her hand touched my thigh.

She grabbed one of my hands and pushed my palm down flat against her leg.

My lips kept kissing her.

My lips said: "Stop."

Her fingers continued crawling along the surface of my jeans.

"Cecilia," I said, "stop."

Cecilia reacted to the word Stop the way most men do—treating it as a set of runway lights saying-telling-commanding them: Keep going, keep doing what you're doing—come on, come on—land right here.

"*Cecilia*. Stop."

"Okay," she said.

But not okay, because still she . . .

Enough!

I pushed her away—far enough away that her lips left my lips and her body left my body, and her fingers left my body.

She looked at me with sad eyes. "I'm sorry," she said. She looked down.

"You're okay."

"Oh, man, I'm sorry."

"Don't worry about it, Cecilia."

"Can I hug you?"

"Yeah. Sure, of course."

She hugged me.

She started kissing my shoulder.

She pulled my shirt up and tried to start kissing my chest.

"Cecilia."

"Baby."

"Seriously."

Kiss, kiss, kiiiss, and—

"*Cee!*"

—I pushed her off me again.

"Look. I'm sorry," I said. "But . . . "

Cecilia and I sat there.

"We can't have that anymore."

Cecilia and I sat there.

"I can't be with you. I don't *want* to be with you, Cecilia."

Cecilia and I looked into one another's eyes.

She tore her eyes away.

She pushed off the mattress and didn't look back and stormed out of the shack into the cold, unforgiving night.

I sat alone on the mattress. I rubbed my hands over my face.

I got up and left the shack, and I walked down to the water.

* * *

Cecilia cried and looked at everyone but me as she stood at the front and spoke.

I sat beside Jez, and I stared at some anonymous point beyond Cecilia, and I wondered how different the memorial service would be if Lenore was actually here.

I also looked at the empty seat at the end of the front row, and I wondered how different the emotional dynamics would be if Maxwell was actually here...if Maxwell still thought that Lenore was actually dead.

Maxwell was not at the church. He had stayed at The Palace, on Nantucket Island, so he could take Lenore to the tiny airport on Nantucket Island. So Lenore could depart from America and from her old life, never to return.

Jez and I made eye contact again.

Cecilia kept mumbling in eulogy.

Cecilia kept crying.

On the previous night, after Cecilia left the shack—after Maxwell joined me by the water and told me about his time with Lenore, and after he persisted to ask about my night with his sister until I finally offered him a condensed and PG-rated version—I returned to Banucci Manor with dreams of sleep decorating my vision.

Inside, I found a note from Lenore taped to the bathroom mirror.

> *Richard.*
> *Wake me up if you feel like it.*
> *~ Lenore*

I considered ignoring the note and instead retreating to sleep, but I realized that neither of these were legitimate options. I folded the note and stuffed it into my pocket, and I took a breath before mounting the stairs.

When I entered Lenore's room I looked at the clock on the wall and saw that it was nearly 3:00. I stepped over the patch of wet moonlight that shimmered over the floor, and I leaned against the bed and whispered in her ear.

"Lenore. Lenore."

Lenore rolled over.

"Lenore."

Lenore opened her eyes.

"Hello, Richard."

"Your note said to wake you up."

"It did."

"Okay. Well . . . "

"What time is it?" she said.

I told her.

"Geez," she said.

"I'm sorry—it's pretty late, huh? Should I not have woken you?"

"No. No." She pushed herself onto her elbows. "I don't mind at all."

"Go back to sleep, okay? Right? You need your rest."

"I'm fine."

"You sure?"

"I'm sure," she said. She yawned. She reached up at the end of the yawn to halfway cover her mouth. "Oh, I'm sorry. So tired."

"Go back to bed, Lenore."

"No, I—"

"I'm sorry for waking you."

"Not at *all*, Richard. Boy-oh-boy, you're just *such* a sweetheart."

"I do my best..."

She pulled a pillow behind her back and leaned back against it. She asked me if I wanted to sit.

I sat on the edge of the bed.

"How did things go with Cecilia?" she said.

"Huh? Oh, I—how did you know about...?"

"Max told me that she dragged you away from him. He said that she seemed a bit upset."

"Well..." I gave Lenore the same condensed and all-audiences-approved version I had given to Maxwell, and she chuckled and shook her head and patted the bed beside her so I could sit closer to her than I was sitting. She started to scratch my back, and she told me the story of her conversation with Maxwell.

Her version of the story was identical to his.

She told me that she was going to skip her memorial service in the morning, and that Maxwell would take her to the airport and send her away from the country. Away from all of this and everything, and the baggage that goes with it.

Why? I asked.

Because, she told me, it was the right thing to do. It was the right thing to do for herself. It was the right thing to do for everyone else.

No more Maxwell—for her to be on the fringes of his life as his silent always-torturer.

No more Jez—for her to cheat on her husband with.

No more Chas to cheat on her.

No more duplicity and pain and emotional anguish.

A chance to start over, right back at the place from which she had begun.

And hey, she said, maybe someday I'll see you again. Maybe someday, somewhere, on the other side of the globe. Maybe you will be there, and I will be there also.

Maybe we'll make stories.

Wouldn't it be nice, Richard, for your life to be a story?

You could do that, she told me. She said: I could do that also.

"What do you think about all of that?" she asked.

And this is what I told her: "Lenore," I said, "whatever you decide to do, it's probably the right decision."

I said this because I felt that she was making the right decision—the *only* decision that would take her away from all her potential suitors, from all her past and present and future loves, extricating her from the desolation that she was wont to create. Allowing the world to heal. Allowing life to continue.

The more good things that happen, the easier it is to forget about that one good thing that didn't.

And so, Lenore and I talked for a while longer, and then I kissed her forehead. I fell asleep beside her.

These were the things I thought about as Cecilia spoke at the front of the church, during Lenore's memorial service.

Cecilia stopped speaking, and she wiped away tears and set the microphone in the microphone stand. She struggled toward her seat, leaving the front of the church open to the final eulogizer of the day. Lenore's unfaithful husband: Mr. Charles Montana Jr.

Chas mumbled on for a while, and clear rivulets trickled down his face and fell from the sides of his chin, hitting the floor with the pinpoint of a *plop*, and finally his voice choked up and he stopped speaking altogether. The microphone slipped from his fingers.

The microphone landed with a *thunk!* amongst his tiny pond of tears, and he stumbled toward the back.

* * *

Looking back on that day, I realize that Jez was the only person in the church whose eyes followed Chas all the way to the door. Everyone else adhered to a common set of propriety-conscious decency, giving the man a furtive glance before shooting their eyes forward again.

Not Jez. No, Jez sat beside me, and his back pressed against me as he craned his neck and craned his shoulders and eventually craned his entire torso around, marking each step of Chas's journey with intensity the levels of which can be born of only one thing: An irreversibly vested interest; a high-stakes correlation between oneself and the actions of another.

The minister rushed forward on quick little feet, and he snatched the microphone up from the floor. He ran one of his restless hands through his thinning gray hair, and he coughed and *ahem*ed and generally did the best he could to ease the mood in the church without managing to ease it at all.

"Oh, ahhh—*ahem*—yes, let us all bow our heads. Ah yes, oh—let us bow our heads before the good Lord in silent supplication—ah; oh—to His spirit of comfort. Ah, okay—yes, yes," and his hand tickled along his head again, "such is the way of grief, but the Lord provides for comfort in—ah, oh, hmmm yes—times as difficult as these."

The people bowed their heads, and I started to bow my head, and I felt Jez lurch forward beside me.

He's about to leave, I thought.

I felt my hand move.

He's about to follow Chas.

My hand touched his leg. My fingers squeezed—only a small amount, only enough to grab his attention—and for the rest of my life I'll regret this seemingly innocuous reaction.

When I squeezed, Jez snapped his head forward, and his eyes cut toward me. Our eyes met. I gave his leg another little squeeze—hoping to evoke a measure of reassurance—and I nodded toward the front.

Jez nodded too.

Jez closed his eyes and bowed his head, and I did the same.

By the time the minister finished allowing us silence, then started praying, then finished praying, a chain of unchangeable events had been set in motion.

How Much.

Forever realigning everything in our lives.

* * *

When the minister finished praying we lifted our heads once more, and Jez turned again. His body paused for one or two seconds as his mind processed what his eyes must have been yelling, then he shot out of his seat and slipped from the pew and shuffled down the aisle—his head lowered a marginal degree, as if such a concession would make his departure somehow more acceptable or somehow less noticeable.

I waited for several seconds before standing as well and following in his wake.

The sun was bright when I stepped outside. The door of the church bumped shut behind me, and I squinted. A slight breeze rustled my skin. I waited for my eyes to adjust as I breathed the frigid, December afternoon.

Jez stood at the bottom of the tiny hill—the hill on which the church rested; the hill whose grass looked cold; the hill whose middle was incised with a straight, concrete path, the path appearing from a distance as though it ran from the mouth of the church like a thin, gray tongue. Jez lingered at the base of this path with his fists clenched. The muscles in his neck were tight. My eyes adjusted gradually to the brightness of the bleak and tragic day, and these were the things I saw—

I saw how the wind struggled to tousle Jez's impeccable hair; I saw how Jez's hair won the battle.

I saw how the clouds looked like large balls of cotton.

I noticed the crispness in the air.

I saw that the tiny little town—and the entire world along with it—was utterly indifferent to our mournful gathering. I saw that no one cared, and I saw that I did not care either, and I saw that there were a thousand other funerals in other parts of the world, all going on at the exact same time, and I saw that the only things any of us ever see are the things directly before us.

I did not see the car until it was already too late.

Jez had stepped into the street—his feet pacing, his mind wandering. Jez looked everywhere and saw absolutely nothing. Jez clenched his fists tighter.

The car flew forward in a flash of bright yellow, and I thought for one moment some formless set of thoughts, thoughts that molded into words would go something like this: That car is moving fast; that car is moving *too* fast; that car is going to hit.

That car is going to hit.

That car is going to . . .

Oh my goodness.

I lunged forward from the concrete landing at the top of the steps at the end of the path. At the top of the hill.

And my voice yelled: "Jez!"

Jez turned.

Jez saw the car.

The world blurred—the metal and man merging for a fantastic, magnificent, catastrophic moment—then time slowed as Jez defied gravity for a pair of twisting seconds.

His shoulder hit the windshield.

His face hit the hood.

His legs spun above him, and his head danced with the metal as he moved one way and it moved the other—a fractional space of cold, rushing air separating the two.

The car moved on, and Jez landed. His face met the ground with a sickening noise whose spelling I cannot create.

Somewhere, a clock ticked.

Somewhere, the world kept turning, totally indifferent.

Jez skidded across the pavement for a miniature window in the space of eternity, and he came to rest with a spray of blood laid out before him.

I stood still, and I stared.

Somewhere, time disappeared.

Somewhere, inside me, my ears rang loudly. Beneath that, I heard an enormous crash.

My eyes moved quickly.

My eyes absorbed the scene—

What once had been a car, and once had then been a flash of destructive yellow, was now obsolete. The brick wall had won, and the car spun out in a compact reincarnation of its original garish self.

The world kept spinning.

The holocaust was complete.

CHAPTER 9

These several months later I remember the rest of that day, and that night and the next day, only as a circulating wheel of white rooms and wet eyes and light that seemed always to be entirely too bright.

It is never until tragedy strikes that the world takes notice. And even then humanity's interest is fleeting and unstable— their attention standing on fidgeting feet in a single spot for a single moment until something more current happens, and their feet shuffle on. And I think: If it is only through constant tragedy that we can achieve any sort of continuing recognition, where then does that leave us all, who each have but a single life to spare?

Lily was pronounced dead at the scene. Her neck snapped forward when the car hit the wall, and the bones in her face broke inward and sliced through her brain.

Jez was not so fortunate.

The ambulance arrived five minutes later, and in the forever-space of 'meantime' I sat in the street and held Jez's hand as the blood spilled from his face, climbing my pant legs and clinging to my skin. I tried to whisper to him over the noise.

Shhh, I told him. Shhh, I said, it's all okay.

Inside the ambulance—

Things beeped, and the EMTs fooled around with a variety of devices. They touched Jez all over and said things to each other, and I noticed almost none of this as I bent over him and leaned in close and tried to keep telling him that things were all okay.

Shhh . . .

His groans and his whimpers. His tangible pain. Lingering in the air like a heavy scent.

Shhh, Jez. Shhh.

The ambulance weaved through the streets, and it felt as though we were trapped in a barrel as it shot down rapids. Boom and bang and back-and-forth.

It's all okay, Jez.

Just before we arrived at the hospital he clenched my hand tighter. A couple of his fingernails dug deeper into my skin.

I wanted to pull away, but I didn't.

Shhh.

"Rich."

"Shhh. Jez, don't talk."

"Rich."

The EMTs yelled things that turned into a muddle of undecipherables by the time they reached my ears. Maybe they were still yelling to each other, or maybe they were yelling at Jez, or maybe they were yelling at me.

"It's all okay, Jez—it's all okay, bud. Just be quiet, just stay still."

"Richard, Richard, come down here."

"Shhh, no no, it's all okay."

"Come down here, Rich."

His once-beautiful face looked like a pile of mashed meat. Gauze concealed half of it, and the other half was red. The brilliant red of death.

His eyes bulged out of his skin.

"Rich!" he yelled, and his yell was coarse.

I leaned in close to him. As close as I could make it.

"My pocket, Rich. Reach in . . . in my po—in my pocket." A little fountain of blood bubbled up in his mouth and spilled over, racing in streams along the side of his face. Slipping onto the gauze where it tangled with the ever-spreading red.

I closed my eyes because I couldn't take it any longer.

I'm pretty sure Jez kept his eyes open. He knew that he had no more than a handful of time before he would never open them again.

"My pocket," he fought to say, and this time he coughed at the end. A small shiver of blood jumped up and clung to my face, and I didn't wipe it away.

"Jez," I said. I said: "Shhh," but none of that helped.

"Po—" *cough! cough!* "—pocket."

"Jez," I said. I put my hand on his chest.

He screamed. His scream touched the far ends of the scale and turned my blood to ice.

"Jez, I'm sorry! Augh, God. Shhh—"

"*Aoooough!*"

More yelling from the EMTs.

More beeping.

More—

"The pocket! My po—"

Cough. Cough. Cough.

The ambulance ripped through traffic, and in a strange flash of lucid thought I saw the outside perspective we always experience when an ambulance shoots by. How we think of having to pull over. How we think of the inconvenience. How we think of all the puny things in our own puny world.

How we never think of what's going on inside the faraway confines of that terrible little box.

"*Auuuuugh!*" He reached up with blood-soaked palms and found my shirt, and he gathered handfuls, and he yanked me toward his face. "Pockets, Rich!" He struggled to breathe. He said to me again—one last time—"... *pockets.*"

The ambulance slowed. The EMTs started bustling. I plunged my hand into one of his pockets and my hand came up empty.

I reached over him—careful to keep all my weight off his chest, off any other part of his decimated body—and when I disappeared into this pocket my hand touched paper. I gripped the paper. I yanked it out. The EMTs ignored me while the ambulance lurched and they opened the doors and everything moved outside and across the pavement and into the hospital, and I stood still.

I watched.

I unfolded the paper—elaborate stationary; felt like dried flowers—and after I read it I shoved it into my pocket.

I stood still a while longer. Processing. Drowning.

I came alive, and I rushed around to the front of the hospital.

The Montanas: Just arriving.

"How is he!" Mamma Montana screeched.

"I need your keys!"

"What?"

"Your keys!"

"Oh!"

She threw me her keys.

I dove inside her car and gunned the engine, and I followed the map that Lenore had drawn for Jez.

I arrived at the bike trail on the other side of the town. I got out of the car, and I jogged. I climbed the hill. I followed the instructions that Lenore had written.

The note told Jez that she was still coming to the funeral. Look for her, it said. She would sit near the back. She would wear a black veil. Look for her. She would meet him afterward, at this spot off the bike trail. She would meet him, and they would leave together.

I reached the spot.

I looked around.

Nothing.

I sat. I read the note again.

I folded the note and put it in my pocket, and I hiked down the hill and stumbled down the bike path.

I returned to the hospital in a haze of unreality.

Maxwell was just arriving when I parked and climbed out.

"She wasn't there," he said to me.

"She wasn't there either," I said.

Cecilia burst out of the hospital and didn't look at either of us.

Mamma Montana trailed out behind her.

"He didn't make it," she said. She cried harder.

Nada y pues nada.

Nothing and then nothing.

* * *

The following days were bleak and depressing.

The rest of the world prepared for the materialistic merry-making of one more soon-to-be-lost Christmas, but for us...

...for us, another funeral swept us along in its turbulent currents, and another wave of people who did not know the departed crashed upon The Palace and ate expensive food while they talked to everyone and listened to no one. I heard one man make a joke to an equally inauthentic acquaintance—

"Well hell, if things keep going at this rate, this'll become our second home."

—and both men laughed.

I set my jaw tight and left The Palace, and I returned to Banucci Manor. I wondered if there was some way—any way at all—to escape this souring life.

"Where did things go wrong, Richy?"

"Whoa, Maxwell—what are you doing over here?"

"Had to get away, brother—haaaad to get away."

"Yeah?"

"Yup. You?"

"The same," I said. "Say, you want to go inside?"

"No no, man—brother—I'm fine out here. You join me?"

"Sure. Give me one minute."

I slipped inside and went to my room and rummaged around until I found a sweatshirt. I pulled the sweatshirt over my head, then I decided to grab my coat as well. The night was quite cold.

Maxwell was wearing a T-shirt.

I returned to the back porch and sat down beside him.

"Let's go out near the point," he said.

"Okay," I said, "let's go out near the point."

Maxwell stood, and I stood too. I followed him across the grass and to the street and up the street until we reached the entrance to the point.

We chose our spots in the sand—the same ones we'd sat in several nights earlier, on the eve of Lenore's memorial service; the same ones Cecilia and I had sat in that same night as well, talking to each other for what would likely become the last time ever—and Maxwell smoked a cigarette and stared at the sky.

He told me that he didn't care about Lenore having lied to him. "No no, brother—it's no big deal. I understand, man. She was confused, it happens. She thought she had figured out, oh, uh—figured out where she belonged and all, but we all do that, we all make mistakes. But I don't mind, see, because I can see me in that same situation. I can see me doing the same thing."

On the morning of the memorial service, after all of us left for the mainland, Maxwell waited for an hour before walking over to Banucci Manor, just like Lenore had told him to do. He showed up, looked around, and Lenore was not there. He had to wait for the next ferry before he could leave the island.

"But I can respect that—I can *laugh* at that, brother—because that's so *much* like me. Oh, so damn much, and it makes me smile—I can't lie about that, it does, it makes me smile—and I don't mind at all."

"Okay," I said.

"What?"

"Nothing."

"She's coming back, you know?"

"Okay," I said again.

"I know you don't believe me, Rich—and that's okay, brother. That's okay, I really don't care. I know what I know, though, and I know she'll come back. You don't believe me?"

"I . . . "

"Maybe you don't, and that really is fine. But you'll see, Richy—she'll be back for me. You'll see—we're meant to be together. It's the way this story ends."

And I watched Maxwell cling to the shards of misplaced hope—the shards of faith in a humanity whose distinguishing features are duplicity and deceit—and he sank and sank deeper, and he drifted further from the shore, always believing that something would someday save him. That something would someday change.

Always believing in the ever-imagined goodness of an ever-failing humanity.

* * *

Wilson Wrentsom never found out about the affair in which his wife had been a member—for Mr. Wrentsom, his wife's sudden breakdown seemed utterly and indescribably indefinable.

Had he been privy to the story in all its shameful entirety, he might have reacted differently.

Had Mr. Wrentsom known the truth—had he known of his wife's infidelity; had he known the identity of the man with whom she'd been unfaithful—he might not still be working for Montana Inc., putting in his fifty hours each week and running around in circles as he struggles with all within him to climb up the ladder.

Last I heard, Mr. Wrentsom applied for the corporate job vacated by Jez.

Oh, the irony if he actually wins it.

What Lily told her husband on the afternoon of the funeral was, 'I'll be back in a minute. I'm going to get some coffee.'

And she left the house, and she drove her car into a brick wall and died instantly before she made it home.

The river on which her participation in the story drifts—from the time she left her house to the time she ended her life—I've been forced to piece together from the converging tributaries of eyewitness accounts and rational assumptions.

The eyewitnesses said they saw a yellow car in the parking lot on the far side of the park. They said the driver was female— 'Blonde, attractive . . . yeah, it was the girl who drove into the wall, same girl, I'm sure of it'—and they said that she stared toward the church as though she was blocking out the entire world. As though she was focusing on the pinpoint of an idea as she willed it into existence.

As Lily waited—as she probably pressed the gas sporadically and sometimes pounded the wheel—the door of the church eased open. And there he was—Chas.

Chas walked down the hill, and he looked both ways, and he crossed the street. When he reached the bench on the edge of the park he lowered his face to his hands.

Lily pressed the gas again.

Lily pounded the wheel.

Lily was about to climb out of the car and walk across the grass—was about to approach her lover with a thousand words chasing themselves in circles around her brain, with not even a single one resting on her tongue—was about to commit herself to resolving this entire debacle when the door of the church eased open once more. And out stepped a woman. The woman walked down the hill and looked both ways, then she crossed to the park and sat down beside him.

No way, Lily thought. No way, it can't be—it . . . it's not possible.

Lily pressed the gas.

Lily pounded the wheel.

Lily put the car in reverse and backed up and put the car in drive, then she left the parking lot and drove away from the church, hoping to escape everything that was destroying her life.

Coffee—yes, coffee. Pick up some coffee and drive home to your husband.

But no, she thought. But oh, she thought. Let me circle around for just one last look.

Lily was exactly four minutes from the church when she decided to return. She pulled into a driveway—

"She pulled into my driveway," the man told the news that night. "We were expecting my wife's parents—they came in from South Carolina, and . . . well, they don't have cell phones, so we weren't sure what time they'd be here, hadn't heard from them yet—and I heard a car pull into the driveway, so I went to the window to look. It wasn't them—they got held up with some friends in Baltimore, so they didn't make it up here till later in the day—but the car in the driveway was this bright yellow car, with this pretty little blonde lady driving it, who—well, you know, it was the same girl. It was our driveway she turned around in, I saw her just as she was pulling back out."

—and by the time she reached the church again, Chas was gone. By the time she reached the church again, Jez was outside.

By the time Lily returned she had lost sight of all the things that keep each of us sane and grounded in reality.

Lily pounded the wheel and pressed the gas harder, and she barreled forward—determined to teach Chas a lesson.

But oh, Lily—wait.

But oh, Lily—stop.

But oh, Lily—that isn't Chas. Lily, that's Jez. Lily, slow down.

But Lily—forever and always, and so on to infinity—never realized that Chas was away. Never realized that Chas was gone.

None of us realized Chas was gone.

Didn't realize until much too late.

* * *

As I've drifted further from that day, it has become to me like a skyscraper on the landscape of my past. Other things have faded off with the distance—the flowers and plants of mundane memories now disappeared from sight—but that particular day, the day of the memorial service for the woman who wasn't dead, has become more and more clear, standing out against the horizon like a monolithic monster that reminds me always of the unreality of reality.

The final piece of the puzzle arrived on the morning of Jez's funeral—a package, shipped to Banucci Manor. Care of Richard Parkland. To be delivered to Jez Tagsam.

I took the box inside and opened it at the kitchen table.

Inside of the box—the punt boat.

Dear Jez.

I would like to begin by telling you that I'm sorry. I am sure you're upset, and I hope you believe me when I tell you that I deeply regret the pain you must be feeling.

If you must know the truth, I needed to get away.

I never lied to you, Jez, I hope you believe me when I say that. I truly did intend to meet you at the hill off the bike trail as soon as the memorial service ended. I intended to carry out the plan on which we had decided, and I intended for the person beside me right now to be none other than you.

I was at the memorial service, you know that. I think I saw you looking at me several times throughout. I was there, and I watched everything.

If I am to be totally honest, I thought that you would have followed Chas when he left the church. I am still shocked that you didn't, Jez, I really thought you would have. I cannot say for certain, but perhaps things would be different right now if you had.

You did not follow him, Jez.

But I did.

It surprised me when you did not show up outside with us. Jez. Oh, Jez, I am most terribly sorry.

Chas walked outside, and he looked both ways and crossed the street, and I slipped outside and followed him. He sat on a bench, and he held his face in his hands. He was crying, Jez, he really was. He was really torn apart.

You know that I love you, my dear. I always will. Nothing will ever change that, and I hold within me nothing but the fondest of memories of all our moments together.

But nothing is ever concrete, my love. Nothing at all. And when I went outside and looked both ways and crossed the street myself, I approached my husband with a brain full of words and with nothing at all on my tongue.

I did not need anything on my tongue.

I sat down beside him, and I touched his shoulder. He refused to even look up. Oh, it was positively tragic. He was so broken apart, so downtrodden, over my death, I, well. Jez, I don't quite know how to explain it. The change that overtook me. I felt my hands reaching up, and I didn't know what they were doing.

They were removing my veil, Jez, the veil that hid me from the truth. The veil that kept me dead to everyone at my funeral.

I said my husband's name, and he looked at me, and there was no turning back.

I do love you, Jez. I do hope you know that. But Chas is my husband, and of course I love him too.

I know that he sometimes is not the man he wishes he could be, but oh how he wishes. And it breaks my heart to see it, Jez, you should see it. He really does try to do right, see. And he really does love me.

It's the way things must be, dear. I hope you see that.

And no matter what happens in your future, and no matter what happens in mine, we can always look back separately and still be together. Always look back and know:

We will always have Nantucket.

All my love and all my best.

Yours forever and truly,

 ~ Lenore

I folded the note and slipped it back into its bed of red velvet in the bottom of the punt. I slid the little lid back over the little compartment, and I walked to the water and stood on its edge for several empty minutes. I reared back. I launched the punt out into the ocean where it landed and sank and disappeared forever.

I returned inside the house, and I went back into the kitchen, and the cracked pole was on the floor. It had fallen from its place alongside the tragic souvenir, and I picked it up and thought of taking it to the ocean and getting rid of it as well.

Instead, I slipped the cracked pole into one of my bags.

It is sitting on my desk right now, beside my computer as I type this.

Somewhere, time passes, and somehow these things matter.

* * *

It's been four months now.

I've heard rumors, of course. I've heard stories about Chas and Lenore, about their extravagant excursions throughout the whole of Western Europe. I've come in contact with people who claim to have dined with them in Rome, or to have danced with them in Venice. I've attended gatherings where their names became the central focus of clustered discussions—'Oh, *such* a lovely couple, the both of them are just pos*itive*ly pleasant'—and I've been forced to listen as Chas and Lenore's aura of perfection is lauded and adored by pockets of misguided travelers.

This afternoon I took lunch with a friend of mine in the city—Ricardo, from Italy, who claims that he and I were separated at birth—and he mentioned a dinner party he attended right here in Paris not three nights ago.

"Oh," he said, speaking with his hands and waving about his flamboyance like a flag on top of a mountain, "and this *one* couple in *especially*, oh—ah—Rich old boy, you should have *seen* them. Most lovely couple *alive*."

"Yes?"

"Oh yes! With the grandest tales and stories of absolute great—I tell you, friend, you have got to meet them both. Oh, and the girl—" and at this he kissed his fingers and released the kiss to the air, as if he was a bad actor in a bad American movie, trying to capture Sicilian purity in a Hollywood snapshot.

"Good-looking, huh?"

"Like you would not, oh, *believe*. Absolute gorgeous."

"Oh yes," I said, and I sipped my espresso.

"Lenore," he said,

"Excuse me?"

"Lenore. That was the lady's name. Such a *beeeeautiful* name, no?"

I tossed my money onto the table and stood.

"Where are you go to, my friend?"

I wandered along the bank of the river, then I trickled through the streets.

Aimlessly.

Incessantly.

My feet moving me forward.

I watched the swell of humanity on which the city drifted— picking apart the uniquenesses and singularities of every individual.

I recognized that all of these people, no matter how different, were all exactly the same. They each breathed, they each labored, they each struggled through life.

Alive.

And what a trial it was.

My legs began to tire and my feet began to ache, and I found myself standing in front of 10 rue Delambre, where so many buried years ago the Dingo Bar resided. Open all night. Offering to the artists and artisans of this city a place in which to gather and pour upon each other the contents of their venerable minds.

The year was 1925, and inside the doors of this selfsame inanimate structure Ernest Hemingway met F. Scott Fitzgerald.

The brilliance of one man's career began, and the brilliance of another's began to crumble.

The fragility of a gift.

The fragility of a dream.

I pictured the Dingo Bar alive once more, buzzing with thoughts and ideas and genius—the minds of the Paris night carried through life on the illuminant optimism of an unobtruded future.

I thought of the question Ricardo had asked: 'Where are you go to, my friend?'

Where . . .

Such a poignant question.

Where . . .

If only I knew the answer.

* * *

On my last night in Nantucket, with my bags packed and waiting for me beside the front door, I walked through the house and examined all the things I'd been living with for weeks. I looked at walls, and I imagined Lenore's eyes passing over the same contours and spaces. I touched doorframes and sat in chairs. I breathed deeply, imagining her scent.

I entered the bedroom in which Lenore had stayed. The sheets washed, the bed made. The last traces of Lenore, tidied away into nonexistence.

Lenore and Jez, lying on the bed together. Kindling the flame she'd ignited within him so many years before.

I went outside that final night on the island, and I laid in the sand with an open sky above me and a wind dancing into me. The waves hit the sand and ran forward before falling back upon themselves and starting over again. The incessant beauty of existence.

I drifted back through time until I saw the island in its virgin state, rising green and rocky for the eyes of Captain Gosnold. This jewel of tranquility amongst the turbulent Atlantic—What must he have thought?

I imagine that he paused a moment, not speaking, not breathing. Thinking deep within himself: This is a place for dreams.

A dream is what Jez subsisted on. A dream is what he chased.

Jez believed in something I myself have lost sight of: An unwavering faith in the fulfillment of life.

I cannot help but wonder whether the trail of destruction that snakes undulating behind Lenore is a wondrous study in the pursuit of such ideas.

Each of us is borne along this rushing river of life, pushed forward and tugged along and sometimes dunked under, with our dreams forever receding before us, forever calling us onward, forever eluding our grasp.

But that's no matter, for there is always tomorrow. We will run with heads held high and arms stretched farther . . . forever believing that someday— —

And still the clocks keep ticking, and still the world turns. And time disappears with laudable indifference to the existence of us all.

ABOUT THE AUTHOR

JM Tohline grew up in a small town just north of Boston. He lives in a quiet house on the edge of the Great Plains with his cat, The Old Man And The Sea. *The Great Lenore* is his first novel. You can find him online at www.JMTohline.com.